Soulmate:
"A Romance of Dysfunctional Proportions"

Also by Kerry Wood

#FakeNews MSM: The Illegitimate Press

Soulmate:
"A Romance of Dysfunctional Proportions"

KERRY WOOD

ADVANCED PRINTING AND GRAPHICS
2020

ISBN 978-1-7353622-0-5 (paperback)

Advanced Printing and Graphics
26 Angela Circle
Inman, SC 29349

www.kerrywood.com

Our books may be purchased in bulk for promotional, educational, or business use.

Ordering Information:
U.S. trade bookstores and wholesalers:
Please contact APG email me@KerryWood.com.

First Printing: February 2, 2020
Printed in the United States of America

Dedication

This book is dedicated to the one and only who ever actually held my heart. I believe the stars had to truly align to bring us together, that fate definely had a hand in things, and that time has mattered little, with us belonging to each other long before we even met, and our hearts continuing to belong together long after your departure. The loss of you, my best half, has left me with nothing but grief. You made me a better person, I'll forever miss you, continuously hoping to see you on the other side. 1432

And to the memory of my best friend:

Truman

01/01/2004 – 06/9/2019

Preface

I'm struck with irony as I sit here, contemplating what to write as a Preface. This is where authors will typically share their own thoughts about the work that follows and I don't know that I can ever realistically do that. Even though this is just my second book, I've been writing most of my life. I've written college courses, instruction manuals, scripted radio and television commercials, hundreds of small articles for publication, and all of it has always come relatively easy to me. This book was something I felt I had to do. It wasn't a labor of love. Putting these words to paper was one of the most painful exercises I've ever endured. While the story is fiction, I struggled every single day I worked on this, recalling how much my lost soulmate meant to me. I wanted to put a piece of "us" in the book while also using it as a tool to help me cope with a loss that I'm not sure I'll ever come to terms with.

No one should ever have to go through life without their best friend and lover, feeling as though you are always cheating when you're with another, making it virtually impossible to ever have another real relationship.

All that said, if you find this book to be unexpected, then I feel I accomplished what I set out to do for the readers.

"We loved with a love that was more than love." ~ Edgar Allan Poe

1

When Worlds Collide

An unidentified man lay on a floor, alone in a room enveloped in darkness but for a single light above his head. Slowly, he struggled to stand, then wavered a bit once he was on his feet. The light above his head illuminated the area immediately surrounding him, and no more. Looking out beyond the light, in all directions, he saw nothing. For a brief moment, panic began to wash across him, but he quickly regained his composure.

He yelled out into the darkness, "Hello!" but heard nothing in response. He tried again with, "Is anyone out there?"

He felt a little unnerved at the way his own voice sounded. When he yelled out, the darkness absorbed his words as though he was pouring water slowly into a sponge. There wasn't the slightest bit of echo, and there certainly wasn't a reply from anyone. He continued to yell despite his belief that no one would hear him.

He sat on the floor, he laid down, he stood back up, and he yelled some more. He repeated these motions under the singular light numerous times. He was uncertain of how much time had passed. Was it minutes or hours? He wondered to himself, reluctant to leave the security of the light and wander off into the darkness.

More time passed, and he convinced himself that he couldn't

remain where he was, and that moving in any direction would be a better decision than staying put, so he stepped out of the light and quickly disappeared into the darkness. No more than twenty paces from the light, he placed his hand in front of his face and couldn't see it. He could feel his heart begin to race. He despised the feeling of being so afraid, that it quickly turned into anger at himself for not maintaining control of his fears.

He shouted out, "Hello, is anyone there?" Nothing. "I need this place to be lit up! And I need it to be lit up now!" he yelled with rage.

Like daylight entering over a horizon, the darkness began to fade as light slowly consumed a very large area surrounding him. Feeling confused, the man began looking in all directions for a clue as to which way to proceed. Where everything had seemed completely black before, it was replaced with the opposite. The floor was a shiny, bright white, as though it was brand new, with no blemishes or marks anywhere that he could see, and it gave him the feeling that he was in a sterile environment.

He continued to look around, hoping to find a wall, and perhaps a door or window. It was like he were alone in a giant warehouse. He could see a couple hundred yards in every direction, and all was open space. Nothing existed, no columns or any other infrastructure, just the light and bright white floor. It took him a few moments to realize that beyond the light remained darkness, and that he now had a much larger space but remained surrounded by an abyss. With the bright white floor below and bright light above, both stretching out so far from him, he could just see the darkness, in the distance, as a small gap between the two, and it created a border that surrounded him on all sides. He was uncertain if he should feel better or worse about his situation.

The man picked a direction and began to walk. As he approached the border of darkness, he stopped with more than fifty feet of space remaining. He sensed something or someone was there. He stared intently and tried to listen for any sounds. Even though he could see and hear nothing, he was becoming more convinced by the moment that someone or something was approaching, and he began slowly stepping backward.

He froze where he was when he noticed a hand breaking the pane of darkness from the other side. Slowly the hand of a woman extended from the dark, followed by a forearm sleeved by a white garment, then she stepped completely into the light and stopped to look at him. His hands began to tremble at the sight of her, and a smile consumed both their faces.

Ten years later, Kenneth Wilson was driving on a winding road, late at night, in his sporty red Corvette ZR1, while thinking about the day he'd just experienced. He was a partner in an architectural firm, and they were left with no choice but to downsize after some major industries within the county had relocated to other states, essentially shutting down the potential of any new development in the immediate area. Ken wouldn't be without work, he would just be without the cool office space, which he had designed for the firm nearly fifteen years ago. He loved that office and had enjoyed going to work there every day since they had constructed it. Now, he would work from home for the foreseeable future. The firm would continue to hold the property as an asset, but eliminating the overhead of keeping the building up and open would mean all the difference in saving the company long term.

After Ken had emptied his office area of personal belongings, which were currently riding in a box in his passenger seat, Ken had attended a little party at the home of one of the firm's other partners. He had a little to drink, but not too much, and it was more the aggravation of the day skewing his judgment behind the wheel than it was any substance in his system. Even though there were signs indicating a hairpin turn, they just didn't register with him until it was too late. He let off the gas and was breaking, but the back end of his car fishtailed around the curve, and as he was trying to regain control of the situation, he found himself staring, imminently, into another set of oncoming lights, joined by the sound of dueling screeches.

The chaos of lights and sounds seemed to be the last thing that Ken could recall as he sat up in bed at the crack of dawn, dwelling on the close call he'd experienced a few hours earlier. He jumped to his feet and looked out his second-floor bedroom window, to his driveway below. There sat his beautiful, shiny, ZR1, with not a scratch on it. "Wow, I was lucky!" he murmured aloud to himself.

As he was looking out his window, he noticed a couple standing outside of the house next door. He was a bit surprised as he hadn't even realized anyone had moved in. He noticed a man in a uniform was yelling at the woman, and with the sound of the conversation being muffled by his closed window, he couldn't make out all that was being said, but he deciphered enough to understand statements like, "you stupid bitch! What were you thinking?" and "you were never anything but trouble! Good riddance!"

Ken tossed on some clothes and shoes, then walked downstairs and out his front door, half thinking he should get involved so the situation didn't escalate into some sort of physical abuse. By the time he made it outside, there was just the woman, standing outside alone, and the uniformed man was nowhere to be found. Ken walked over to introduce himself, and when the woman looked up at him and said "hello," his heart instantly melted.

She stood tall, about 5' 9" to Ken's nearly 5' 11" and she had an athletic build with thick, shoulder-length, dark hair, laced with strands of gray, which gave her a salt and pepper look that Ken found both sexy and irresistible.

"Are you okay?" Ken asked a bit timidly.

"Oh, I'm fine," she replied with a smile, backed up by a bubbly personality that instantly lit a fire inside of Ken, as she put her hand out to shake his. "I'm Amelia Hart, by the way, but most people call me Amy."

"Well, Amy… my name is Kenneth, but most people call me Ken. Welcome to the neighborhood," he said as he reached out to accept her hand. "Amelia Hart? Sounds a lot like Amelia Earhart, so that'll be easy to remember."

Amy produced a fake smile, indicating she had heard the Amelia Earhart comparison too many times, and said, "And that's why I have people call me Amy."

Ken was a handsome man at fifty, with a mature and gentle look about him. He was mostly gray and balding, and had been athletic most of his life, leaving him with a young and toned body. Amy immediately found him attractive.

They stood outside and continued to talk for nearly two hours. She did most of the talking, telling him all about the divorce she was going through and bad dates she'd recently been on, laughing and joking about all of it. Ken found himself not wanting the conversations with her to end and was confused by an uncertainty of just why he felt so drawn to her, as mesmerizing as a flame to a moth. As they departed, she said, in a very childlike and innocent voice, "Will you be my friend?"

For some reason, those words struck a chord in Ken, hearing such juvenile innocence from the mouth of a forty-year-old. Ken knew he would have to get to know this wonderful woman better, and replied, "Of course I'll be your friend," and he walked back home, unable to get those last words and the way they were spoken out of his mind.

A couple of days went by, and Ken couldn't remove Amy from his thoughts, so he went next door to check on her late one evening. She was dressed in comfortable clothing and sporting a baseball cap on her head. Conversations ensued, and he told her that he'd really like to spend more time getting to know her.

"I don't know why," she said. "I must have seemed like a hot mess the other day. I know I rambled about a lot of crazy stuff that would have run most people off."

"Honestly?" he replied. "We laughed and had a good time, but I saw through all that with you."

"What do you mean?" she asked with genuine curiosity, cocking her head slightly to one side.

Ken paused for a moment, then looked her in her eyes and replied, "I saw someone with a lot of pain in their life, desperately trying to distract themselves any way they could. Quite frankly, I recognized it because it's exactly what I've done most of my life."

Amy's head straightened, and her jaw dropped just slightly, as she looked at him in disbelief that he could actually see through her, and Ken knew by her body language that he'd nailed it. She then nervously grabbed the brim of her baseball cap and pulled it down as she also looked downward, attempting to shield her eyes. Ken noted the discomfort his discovery had caused and assured her all was okay.

After a couple of moments, she looked up at him and invited him in. They started on a bottle of Merlot and another two hours of conversation. When the night was over, Ken kissed her for the first time. Amy leaned her head into his, forehead to forehead, and said, "I don't know what I'm supposed to do with you."

"For starters," Ken replied, "maybe we go for a walk or something tomorrow evening when I wrap up my work. Then we can figure it out from there, okay?"

"I'd think I'd like that," Amy said with a sheepish smile.

The next morning, Ken awoke, got ready for the day, then headed downstairs to his kitchen. The floor plan in his home was rather open, and the kitchen area had no real boundaries from the living area. As you looked out from the kitchen, the view was of the back of a flat screen television mounted to a stand with a sofa and a couple chairs just on the other side, facing the TV and kitchen.

As Ken was fumbling around his kitchen, he heard his television turn on and turned to look, then jumped like a startled squirrel as he noticed a man sitting on his sofa. He quickly recognized him, calling out, "Dad? Is that you? What are you doing?"

The man just sat there. Ken walked over to him and walked between his father and the television. "Dad? You okay? What are you doing here this early?"

His father continued to just sit with a blank stare on his face. Ken watched him with curiosity, and after a few moments, his father said, "Ken, I'm so sorry, buddy. I'm so sorry."

A few months ago, Ken's mother had died of cancer and his father had become so withdrawn that Ken had barely seen him. He knew that somehow his father blamed himself for his mother's death, but he had no idea his father was this bad. Ken didn't know what to say, but didn't want to say nothing, so he replied, "It's okay, Dad, nothing is your fault, you know? You just sit here as long as you like, and I'll be here all day if you need to talk or anything. Okay?"

His father just continued to sit there and stare off into space, and it made Ken quite sad to see him like this. Ken waited a bit, hoping for some interaction, but finally walked off and went about his day, making breakfast first, then retreating to his home office. His office area was a little bare because he hadn't used it before today, so he'd never finished setting it up. To one side of the room was a desk with a new iMac on it, a black leather office chair, and a bookcase in the corner with only a handful of books pertaining to his profession along with a leather-bound version of Phantom of the Opera, given to him by the best friend he'd ever had, so he always kept it close by. The walls of his office were bare, and he knew he wouldn't let that last for long.

Ken spent the first part of his day dressing up his office, hanging some pictures, unpacking some books from boxes to fill up the empty shelves, then set up his iMac so he could begin his first project at home. At the end of the day, Ken wrapped up his work, and his mind quickly embraced the anticipation he was feeling about seeing Amy again. Ken walked out into his living area to find that his father had left without ever saying goodbye or anything at all to him.

Ken left his home to visit Amy, and the two headed out into

their neighborhood for a walk. There were twenty-three new homes in the small community, each on one-acre lots, with twenty-one homes remaining vacant, and as they walked the neighborhood, Ken explained that he had designed each of the homes to have some sense of uniqueness inside and out. The way Ken was walking and explaining made it seem to Amy as though it was more like a fun, private little tour, than just a walk.

"So, no one else lives in any of these homes?" asked Amy.

"At least not that I know of," said Ken. "I had assumed all were empty until I spotted you next door. If you had moved into any of the other homes, then I'm not so sure I'd even know you were in the neighborhood."

"Then I'm glad I picked the one next to you," Amy stated with sincerity. "They're all really nice homes, so why is it they are all still empty? And, don't take this the wrong way, but an empty neighborhood like this is a little creepy."

"Yeah... I think it's a lot creepy!" Ken said with laughter. "My firm made a deal with a builder to develop this neighborhood, and before we were even finished, we lost a lot of employers in this town. We lost thousands of jobs overnight, and people began selling homes in the area far below market value so they could sell fast and follow the work, or perhaps move on to another town with better prospects, I guess. Anyway, the housing market dried up fast, and we found ourselves stuck with all these new homes and no real solution to sell them without taking major loses. We've elected to hold on to them until the local housing market turns around. I agreed to take the home I'm in as compensation because my firm was basically too strapped for cash to even properly pay me. And that, as they say, is all she wrote. What's your story?" asked Ken. "I mean, you seem to be at home all the time, right? You don't work, or you don't have to work, or you work from home?"

"I spent many years working for a telecommunications company," replied Amy, "but the company has just been limping along for quite some time and is basically a sinking ship. So, I'm looking for somewhere else to fit in, but in the meantime, I'm getting a nice little settlement in my upcoming divorce so I'm taking my time and being picky. And I'm just trying to enjoy some time off to get to know myself again, if that makes any sense."

"I get it," said Ken as they reached the backside of the neighborhood.

"Wow, that's really pretty," said Amy, looking across a creek which divided the neighborhood from a rustic-looking farm with a home and old barn up on a hill in the distance and a beautiful open meadow full of wildflowers just on the other side of the creek.

The Farm

"Do you think there is a way to cross this creek?" asked Amy with an unusually high level of excitement in her voice. "I really, really, want to walk over there!"

She glanced up and down the creek for a spot to cross before noticing a small walking bridge about thirty yards from them that she didn't seem to notice at first glance. "There!" she blurted like a kid on Christmas day who just found a favorite present. "We can cross over there!"

"And suppose the owner doesn't want us trespassing?" asked Ken, attempting to be practical despite the overwhelming urge to give Amy whatever she wanted.

"We won't know if we don't go ask, silly," replied Amy with a playful smile that Ken could not resist, so they proceeded to the small walking bridge where Amy gleefully crossed the creek, leading the way, and Ken followed her into the open meadow.

Amy danced around with her arms out wide, twirling and laughing, as though she felt free to be herself for the first time in a very long time. Ken watched, taking it all in and thinking about how happy it made him to be with her. After a few moments of dancing around, Amy ran over to Ken, grabbed his hand, giving it a brief squeeze, and pulled him in the direction of the farmhouse. The two of them made their way uphill toward the home, Amy seemingly carefree, while Ken found himself a little nervous at what they might encounter.

On the walk up, Amy rambled in a way that Ken had not seen before. Her entire personality seemed to change right before his eyes. She talked about random things that made little or no sense, and if Ken tried to ask her a serious question, she would ignore him or give the most evasive answer possible. Ken was becoming uncomfortable with her squirrelly personality, mostly because he was uncertain what to do with her. He made two attempts to bring her back down to Earth, but she just became angry and defensive when he tried. He found her behavior truly bizarre and unsettling, but he would just have to let it ride out for now. He wasn't getting turned off to her or thinking any less of her because of the radical change in behavior, but he was honestly becoming concerned for her mental wellbeing.

As they approached the home, Ken could see a man sitting in a rocking chair on a porch. It was clear to Ken that the man was watching them as they approached. Ken lifted his right hand above his head and gave a wave and was certain that the man saw him, even though the man didn't offer to acknowledge. Something felt very off about all of this to Ken, but he couldn't place what was bothering him about this situation, so he continued to walk alongside Amy, who continued to hold his hand and began gripping it a little tighter. Something doesn't quite feel right to her either, Ken thought to himself.

As they approached the porch and Ken was certain they were close enough for the man to hear, he said, "Hello, sir. I'm Ken, and this is Amy. How are you?"

The man just sat for a moment, taking them in with a very curious look. Then he snorted a little from his nose, almost like a small laugh falling short, and said in a slow and deliberate tone, "I've been here nearly a decade. Never had any solicitors before."

"Hush… we're not solicitors," offered Amy in her best, innocent and childlike voice. "We just moved into the neighborhood below and wanted to get to know our new neighbor. I'm Amy and…"

"He said that already," interrupted the man. "That you're Amy and he is Ken, I mean. Tell me, which one of you is responsible for that bridge crossing my creek?"

Amy began shaking her head and stuttering a bit as she said, "Uhhh… we didn't, we don't know, I don't…"

"Probably me," interrupted Ken. "If you're looking for someone to blame, then it'd probably be me."

"Why do you said that it would probably be you?" asked the man. "Do you not know if you're responsible for it?"

"It was my firm," replied Ken in a respectful tone, even though he found the whole topic of the bridge to be odd. "We designed and built the neighborhood below, and I'm the one who signed off on pretty much everything that was done down there. I don't specifically recall anyone requesting a bridge to cross the stream, but I honestly just don't know."

"Then you didn't do it," stated the man emphatically. "I'm Dr. Carson Matthews, by the way. Call me Carson and come on up and have a seat. If you want to get to know your neighbor, then you should take a little time and get to know me. Right?"

Ken and Amy glanced at each other as if they were confirming with one another that it was okay to proceed, then they made their way onto the porch where Carson motioned to a couple of chairs, offering each of them a seat. Ken could tell that Carson was intentionally controlling every last bit of the conversations which followed.

This is a very intelligent man, Ken thought to himself, wondering if he was a good person or not.

Carson had begun by asking questions of Ken and Amy; who they were, where they came from, and how they ended up in the neighborhood below. To Ken, the whole line of questioning felt more like an interrogation disguised as a friendly conversation, but Ken and Amy answered all his questions as politely as they could.

"I really would have thought you two were husband and wife," said Carson with a smile. "You two just look like you belong together."

Ken and Amy exchanged looks again on that sentiment, each uncertain of how to respond. Carson saying that they looked married was the only thing of substance that had come out of his mouth so far that had any real sincerity to it. After that, Carson seemed to relax a little and began talking about himself. Where he did the questioning of Ken and Amy, Ken noticed that he was still controlling the conversation by carefully selecting only what he wanted to share about himself.

Carson shared with them that he had retired a little early in life from being a neurosurgeon, and then he talked about how he had come to this farm nearly ten years ago. He became very somber when he spoke about a woman, and both Ken and Amy knew they had seen no one else at all. "She was the last real visitor I had before you two came walking up. She wondered onto my property, very lost and disoriented. I took her in, and the two of us hit it off right away... much like I suspect you two have."

Carson became silent and looked down at the porch beneath

his feet like he was trying to compose himself. Ken and Amy continued to exchange glances, each time remaining uncertain if they should say anything in response.

After a moment of silence, Carson said, "You know you've achieved a real and lasting love the moment that love turns into a set of swords. You will communicate without words, knowing how the other feels regardless of what's spoken, but it is words and actions which make up the swords. Wise individuals will recognize their best friend and mate for the true gift they are, using their sword to aid and defend the other. The strongest bond is when two wise people behave this way, doing everything in their power to have the other's back. But all it takes is one unwise person in a relationship. One person who fails to appreciate the great gift of a true 'us' and behaves in a selfish manner instead of that of their mate's, or even their own, best interest. When this unwise person turns their sword against the other, it kills passion, destroys trust, and can wreck another human in unimaginable ways. But it doesn't have to be that way, and when two people are right for each other, then often one of them will find the strength to wait out the worst of times, knowing they can come back together, stronger than ever. That's what I had with her. It was ultimately an unbreakable bond."

Then Carson looked directly into Ken's eyes and asked, "To what lengths would you go to hold on to your true love?"

Ken, feeling a little flustered given his newfound feelings for Amy, just replied, "I'm really not sure."

"Then I feel sorry for you," stated Carson with a touch of disdain in his voice. "What you really just told me is that you've never experienced real love for a woman. Sad really, but I think most go through life that way. Missing out. You know? Because when you find the right one—I'm talking, you truly find your match—then you will not want to be without her. People think a real man is one who can march onto a battlefield, or run into a burning building, but that shit is easy compared to what I'm talking about. You march onto that battlefield or run into that burning building planning to come out alive. Wanting to survive it anyway you can while you fulfill your duty. But when you find your one and only, your true love, then you will literally do anything for that person. You will be prepared to sacrifice your well-being and even your life, if that's what's called for. At least that's what Anna meant to me."

Carson again paused and looked down at the porch before he continued, "I loved that woman more than anything in this world, then I nearly lost her. I had to fight a serious battle to get her back. Once I did, we made this place our home, and I had the best five years of my life, right here with her. Even though she's been gone for a while now, I just don't think I can ever bear to leave this place again."

"Gone?" asked Amy softly, as though she was afraid of the answer.

Carson pointed to the side yard where Ken and Amy could see a gravestone, with fresh yellow flowers propped up at the base of the stone.

"And," continued Amy, almost afraid to speak now, "you said you almost lost her before?"

"Isn't the weather just beautiful out here?" asked Carson, putting on a big smile, and clearly redirecting, "You can't help but love it, right?"

Ken and Amy exchanged glances again, as though they each of them were making certain the other was hearing Carson correctly and both were thinking the same thing, did this odd man seriously just change the conversation to weather?

"But you know what I really like?" asked Carson, smiling. "Rain and storms. There is nothing like a good rain to clean the air and the rumbling of thunder to remind you who is still in charge of things. Isn't that right?"

Before they could agree or not, and no sooner did the question leave Carson's mouth, before they heard a distant rumbling of thunder and the sky quickly began to darken. "I'd say that's your cue to head back home," said Carson, putting on an even larger and somewhat creepy smile while looking directly at both Ken and Amy.

"Yes, sir," said Ken as he and Amy got up to leave, both feeling as though they should for reasons other than the weather. Something about the man left Ken feeling rather uncomfortable, almost with a worry that the man could somehow be dangerous if he chose to be.

As they left the porch and began walking across the yard, Carson shouted, "Really was nice visiting with you two. We should do it again sometime." Then he began to laugh rather loudly, and to make things worse, there was a slight echo of his laugh in the air.

Amy looked at Ken and began to giggle a little and said, "That was just a little strange. He was nice, but very, very odd."

"Yeah," agreed Ken, "and what do you think happened with his wife?"

"Maybe she asked too many questions, and he murdered her," Amy said in her best sinister voice, and they both began to laugh.

Amy continued with her squirrelly personality as they made

their way across the farmland. Ken remained quiet, trying to figure out why her personality had changed so drastically. He worried that she was not okay and wanted to figure out how to handle this in case it was something that recurred with her. Not once did the change in personality deter his feelings for her, and he became even more determined to figure it out as part of getting to know her better, and in his mind, continue to work to build a quality relationship.

Walking across the meadow, they each felt a few raindrops, and Amy had to stop and dance for a few minutes in the rain. When they crossed the bridge over the stream, they looked back and could see dark clouds moving in, over the farm, and surrounding the property. Oddly enough, the storm seemed to just be hanging over the farm, and as they walked on home, the weather remained clear and sunny.

Not far into the neighborhood, Amy's personality slowly changed back, and nothing Ken had just witnessed with her personality change was exactly normal, but it wasn't exactly Jekyll and Hyde either. Ken attempted to address odd things she had said while she was squirrelly, but she didn't want to acknowledge any of it. When Ken pushed a little, Amy became very defensive, so Ken backed off, sensing that she was making it clear that she didn't want to acknowledge what had just happened to her. Ken knew by her behavior that something like this had been recurring in her life and that it is something she is not ready or willing to face. He would pay closer attention so he could learn how to handle it at a minimum, or perhaps even help her cope with it one day.

Dear Old Dad

Weeks passed by, and Ken and Amy shared more and more of their lives each day. The two became inseparable and opened up to each other with more of their thoughts and feelings than they had ever shared with anyone before. There was a comfort building between the two, and each knew they didn't want to be without the other.

Because he was continuously worrying about his father, it would often prompt Ken to talk about other members of his family. Even though he would occasionally talk about his deceased mother, he talked the most about his daughter, Wendy, and his sister, Janice. Ken was convinced that with Amy's personality, she would hit it off great with both his daughter and sister.

"I can't wait for you to meet them," said Ken, talking about Wendy and Janice, "and I can't wait to share even more of my life with you."

"I've shared more things with you than most people get out of me in a lifetime," disclosed Amy. "I don't like admitting it, but I do miss you when you're not around."

"Why not admit that?" asked Ken.

"I don't know," said Amy. "There's often a million things I want to say to you, but then I can't find the words."

"You just said that you've shared more with me than most

people get in a lifetime," observed Ken, "but you're also telling me that there's a million more things you haven't said? A million? Good thing we have all of our lives to get that information out of you."

"You know what I mean," said Amy. "Stuff to do with feelings. I'm not good with feelings."

"Like I said," replied Ken with a gentle voice, "we have our whole lives, so I'm not rushing anything."

Ken then began to confide in Amy that he remained about his father. His dad would frequently just be there when he'd get up in the mornings, hanging out on the sofa, watching television, and hardly ever saying a word. Ken could never get him to engage in a conversation, so he was at a total loss of what to do. He thought perhaps if Amy came around more, then a softer touch may get him to open up a little. Amy was all-in for trying, but no sooner did they discuss this, than she fell ill.

"I'm fine," she kept insisting, usually barely able to speak without coughing.

"You're not fine," stated Ken. "You need to rest, so that's what you're going to do, and I'll take care of anything you need."

"I'm not liking this at all," said Amy, squinting her eyes and producing a fake scowl. "I can take care of myself."

Amy remained sick for weeks with cold and flu-like symptoms. Ken's days began to run together. Each morning he would come downstairs in his house and attempt to deal with his father, then he'd run next door to check on Amy. After he finished this morning routine, he'd go back to his home office and work on architectural designs, and it wasn't unusual that he popped in on his father several times a day, always making a failed attempt to engage him. Typically, his dad would just disappear in the afternoon, never saying goodbye or much of anything else, then Ken would wrap up his work and go next door to spend his evening at Amy's house, helping any way he could.

Ken took care of everything around the house. Amy always left the kitchen in a mess, and Ken always cleaned it up. She would always say she felt bad about it, but there was no reason for her to, as Ken enjoyed helping. Ken worked in her yard, turning it into something she came to love, and he painted rooms in her home, helping her redecorate and make everything just the way she wanted.

Amy continued to be sick and very restless. She was growing tired of spending so much time in bed, and it was getting to her. Ken created an area on her screened-in back porch for her to enjoy and relax. He took some strands of clear, white lights and ran them around the perimeter of the porch, up next to the ceiling. With the flick of a switch, Amy's porch became a magical place where she could always retreat and relax.

Ken and Amy began to interact as though they had been married for years. There was just something very natural and normal about the two of them being together. It was effortless, most of the time.

"It's all so seamless with you," Ken explained to her, "like we could just fit together doing anything."

Occasionally, one of them would get triggered by something that reminded them of something negative in a past relationship, but as they began talking these things out, the two of them just continued to grow even closer, each gaining insight and understanding of the other. Ken wanted to know all about her past so he could better understand her and grow even closer.

Often, Amy would say things to Ken which seemed to cut both ways. "I've felt very vulnerable for the last few months around you. You are different from anyone else, and I know that you want to help me and take care of me. I'm just hellbent on trying to make sure that there's a clear distinction between everything, so that you would know that if we are together, it's because I want to be with you and not because I need to be with you or anyone else."

"Who is the anyone else?" Ken asked.

Amy, flustered, said "You know what I mean. There's not anyone else. You know what I mean."

Ken often found her statements a little odd and out of place, but he understood that she really felt helpless in having to rely on him, and that those feelings were difficult on her, truly making her feel vulnerable, which made her uncomfortable. He truly understood these things and did his very best to manage the situations and work through them, with her, as a couple.

After a few weeks, with Amy not getting worse but also not really getting any better, Ken began to grow more concerned by the day, just because it was dragging on. She was refusing to go anywhere for medical treatment, so Ken's thoughts turned to the odd doctor on the farm, behind the neighborhood. Perhaps he would have some helpful suggestions, Ken thought one afternoon, and began walking in that direction.

As Ken approached the farmhouse porch, he noticed Carson was still sitting right where they had left him weeks ago. "Where's your better half?" asked Carson.

"That's the biggest reason I'm here," replied Ken. "Amy has been sick for weeks now. It's cold and flu-like symptoms, and she isn't really getting worse, but she isn't exactly getting better either. With you being a doctor, I was hoping to talk you into coming over and checking her out."

"I can't do that," responded Carson emphatically.

"Why not?" asked Ken, with a defensive tone.

Carson exhaled sharply, and replied, "What I really want to tell you is that I just can't, and leave it at that, but I know you think you love this woman so I don't want to appear too insensitive...so how about this...do you know what agoraphobia is?"

"A fear of leaving your home?" asked Ken, hesitating because he wasn't certain of his answer or where Carson was about to go with this conversation.

"More accurately," stated Carson, "it is a fear of finding oneself in a situation where escape would be difficult or impossible. Thus, people remain at home where they feel they have control. I can honestly say that's the case here. So no, I won't be walking down to your neighborhood."

"Sorry?" said Ken, puzzled by Carson's indifference to his situation with Amy.

"What the hell are you sorry for?" asked Carson, continuing with a rude tone.

"I don't know," said Ken getting irritated, "I guess, sorry that I bothered you? Sorry that you're too screwed up to be able to help the woman I love? I don't know!"

"You would do well to listen to me," said Carson. "It would be good for you, if you developed agoraphobia as well."

"What the hell are you talking about?" asked Ken, bewildered by Carson's statement.

"Let me ask you this," Carson began, answer a question with

a question, "when you guys arrived at my little farm the first time, did you want to stroll on up here, or did she?"

Ken's face looked puzzled as all he could think was, What the hell is this guy talking about or trying to prove? Or is he just nuts?

"That look on your face is rather priceless," said Carson, "but let me tell you this… I know it was her idea to walk up here, just like I know it wasn't you who created that bridge across the creek. And I know you were uncomfortable about coming up here to see me the first time and this time as well. Let me guess… you made yourself do it because she's refusing to go see a doctor on her own? Am I right?"

Ken felt bewildered by this conversation, and he knew it showed, but he remained determined to get something out of Carson, so he asked, "Okay, if you know so much, then what the hell am I supposed to do?"

"Unfortunately, you have the hardest job in the world right now," said Carson.

"And what's that?" asked Ken with a grimace.

"You have to be patient," replied Carson in a matter-of-fact tone. "Now, let me ask you this… is she seeing things?"

"What do you mean by seeing things?" asked Ken, wanting some actual clarification. "What sort of things?"

"I don't really mean anything by it," replied Carson, "just wondering if she is having any sort of hallucinations. That's all."

"Not as far as I know," replied Ken. "I'm guessing that would be a bad thing?"

"Not entirely," said Carson, as though he was intentionally being vague. "It could really go either way at this point. Anyhow. Sorry. Wish I could help further, but I just can't."

"Okay," said Ken, feeling like he'd just wasted time for both of them. "Appreciate it anyway." And he got up to walk off.

"Wait up a minute," said Carson. "You said that Amy was the biggest reason you were here, so there must have been another reason, right?"

"I had thought I'd ask you about my dad as well," replied Ken. "He keeps coming over to my house, and he just sits there, rarely saying anything and will not engage me in any sort of conversation at all. But, if you can't help me with Amy, I don't see how you'd possibly be interested in helping me with him, either."

As Ken was walking off, Carson said, "Look... I'm probably the one who should be sorry, but listen to me on this. Okay? You need to keep Amy close to you and give that gal comfort any way you can. Hold her close and say positive things to her. That's the best you can do right now. My better half got sick like that. Cold and flu type symptoms that went on for weeks before she finally died. I wish I had done more for her...that I could have done more for her. Now, I don't mean to be negative, and I'm sure Amy will be fine, but you must lift her up to ensure it. Okay?"

Ken, with concern on his face, just nodded.

"And," Carson continued, "as far as your dad goes, just sit with him as much as you can. Wait on him to talk and really listen to what he says. Do this, even if what he says makes little sense in the moment or ever makes sense at all. Maybe nothing he says will ever really matter. What matters is that you sit with him and be with him and just listen for when he does talk. That's the best thing you can possibly do in that situation."

Ken put on a fake smile and nodded as if to say "thank you"

without speaking a word, then he walked off, still thinking Carson was an odd bird, but not totally disliking the fellow since he seemed to give some advice, as unhelpful as the advice seemed.

On Ken's walk back to through the neighborhood, all he could think about was how much Amy meant to him. He'd just easily admitted to Carson that he loved her and probably needed to admit that to Amy as well. She was unlike anyone he'd ever had in his life. He was always eager to communicate with her, and it really struck him how every single time she entered a room he had the exact same feeling as the first time he saw her. To him, she was the most beautiful woman in the world, and it didn't matter how many difficulties he'd had with her, his feelings for her and the way he looked at her always remained consistent. He'd never been able to feel like that about anyone before.

4

Falling for You Too

Eventually Amy recovered, for the most part, with just some occasional relapses, and then things settled into a kind of normal between her and Ken. Amy didn't quite know how to handle this newfound relationship as no one had ever treated her so well, been so respectful, and so easy to share her life with. She had told herself that she wouldn't let herself get involved with anyone else for a long time, so she had built in a resistance that she couldn't quite bring herself to defy. She knew the only person holding her back was herself, and the internal struggle she constantly felt around Ken was tearing her apart inside because she couldn't bring herself to accept the relationship for what it was.

Late one evening, Ken was on Amy's back porch with her, which was a frequent occurrence. She was extra nice and more loving than normal. After about an hour, she told him she thought they didn't need to see each other anymore. It was like a blow to Ken, and even though she had pulled back many times, she had never gone down the road of calling it quits. Ken tried asking her why in a variety of ways but couldn't get a straight answer out of her.

Finally, she said, "If it doesn't happen now, then it's going to happen sometime. Maybe next week, three months from now, or next year. At some point it's just going to end, anyway."

Ken didn't know how to respond to that. He realized that on some level she must be very insecure, and he knew that if she would give him a chance, he could eventually prove to her that he will go the distance, and that he fully intended to be there for her from now on. She can't just give up on us for no reason, he thought to himself, there must be something I can do or say.

Ken got up to leave, and Amy stood up and physically turned her back to him so she wouldn't have to watch him go. He hesitated for a moment, then walked up behind her and ran his arms around her waist and pulled her close. She made no effort to get away and leaned her head backward onto his left shoulder. Ken held her for a few moments and could tell she was embracing it. He took his right hand and slowly slid it down from her waist and ran his fingers between her legs. She opened her mouth and began to breathe heavy as her whole body relaxed into his.

She doesn't want to be without me, Ken thought to himself, then grabbed her by her hips, spun her around, gave her a hug, and told her that he would see her tomorrow. He then went home happy, that it wasn't actually over, but concerned about how she kept going back and forth with him.

How can I feel so drawn to someone when I really don't need anyone, she frequently thought, and out loud she often said, "I've never cared about anyone as much as I care about you, including family."

And, as much as her words and actions painted a picture of an internal struggle, she continued to move in his direction as she even told Ken one afternoon, "My dad abandoned me when I was young, then my mother abandoned me, and I don't even really care about that. Ken, you are the first person I've ever actually had in my life that I never want to lose. I know I always want you to be around." And Ken received that statement loud and clear, knowing that no matter what happened between them, he'd always have to find a way to be there for her.

Things continued to develop between the two of them. Ken always making himself available, and Amy always holding back, sometimes a little, and sometimes a lot. Ken became a little frustrated occasionally, but in his mind, he was already planning to spend the rest of his life with her, so was it asking too much for him to be patient if they both had the rest of their lives ahead of them? He didn't think so, and imagined he would travel whatever path he needed to with her, because he had already become convinced that they would be together for the rest of their days, even though, often, it wasn't an easy task for him. One time she began to act indifferent, as if their relationship didn't matter, and Ken asked out of frustration, "So you can just get what we have anywhere, anytime, right?"

"No," she replied, giving him an answer wrapped in a riddle, "I can't get what I have with you from anyone or anytime, and it's not a normal thing. If it was, I would have been able to distance myself a long time ago. For whatever reason, I can't with you, and I can't figure out why."

So, is what we have special enough for her to be with me? thought Ken to himself, or does she actually want to pull away? Why mention you aren't able to distance yourself unless you've been trying?

Feeling a little frustrated, Ken asked if she had ever seen that movie called 50 First Dates. He likened their relationship to that movie, feeling like he often had to start over with her each day. "You're like the Drew Barrymore character," he said.

"Lucy," she replied. "Her name was Lucy."

"So, you've seen it?" Ken asked.

"About a dozen times," she said with enthusiasm. "I love that movie."

After this, whenever she kept pulling back, Ken would occasionally say, "Wake up, Lucy," or "I need you to wake up and come back to me, Lucy."

Their little tug of war had gone on now for months, with two steps forward and one step back. Ken remained patient even though he wanted much more from Amy. Then one night, while having dinner, Amy said aloud, "I wonder just how long we've known each other now?"

Without hesitation, Ken replied in a matter-of-fact tone, "Seven months and five days."

Amy began to laugh, thinking he had to be kidding, that he couldn't possibly know that well enough to just blurt it out. But Ken wasn't laughing, and she quickly realized he must be serious, and asked, "How could you possibly know that?"

"Easy," replied Ken. "Today's date is the 15th, and we met on the 10th, seven months ago. Easy."

"You're such a girl!" said Amy, laughing.

"When things are very important to me, I take note," said Ken with a smile. "There's nothing girly about that."

Amy repeated herself even louder than before, "you're such a girl!" and laughed again.

"Well then," said Ken, "there's something else I've been wanting to say to you, but not sure if it'll scare you or not."

Amy smiled gently, as though she knew exactly what was coming, and she also knew she wanted to hear it more than anything.

"I love you," said Ken for the very first time.

Amy looked serious and replied, "That doesn't scare me… I really care about you. I really, really, care about you."

What the hell is wrong with you? Amy immediately thought to herself.

Their conversations went on for a couple more hours, and Amy would continue to slip in the same words, dozens of times throughout the evening, "I really do care about you," as though she was trying to work herself up to admit what they both instinctively knew.

At the end of the night, as Ken was leaving, he kissed her and it quickly became a very passionate exchanged that went on for several minutes until Amy stopped herself and said, "I don't know what I'm supposed to do with you."

Ken looked puzzled because he truly was, only to hear Amy add, "Meeting you was the best thing that's probably ever happened to me. I don't know what I'd do without you. I really do care about you so much."

Ken smiled, said goodnight, and walked on home. He couldn't help but dwell on the evening with Amy, and how things had been going up to now. He had learned so much about her, getting the impression that she had really allowed herself to open up to him in ways she had never done with anyone else. He knew about some of the traumatic events that had occurred in her life, involving some serious issues with her parents, especially her mother, and getting sucked into a cult environment with her second ex-husband, among other things. As much as she had shared with him, he suspected there was so much more that was causing her to remain cautious in letting herself completely fall for him, as he had already fallen for her.

Ken suspected that she has issues layered on top of other issues. He believed that, at some point, she was likely having difficulty dealing with some sort of trauma when she was hit with another trauma, and perhaps a couple more, altering her behavior each time, taking her off course from normal. Amy had already referred to him as "her rock" frequently. He knew she felt safe and secure with him. He believed them to be kindred spirits, meaning they had very similar personalities, very similar drives, and had endured many of the same pains in life, so they each felt drawn to the other by their ability to completely understand and share themselves. It was unlike any relationship he had ever experienced with anyone.

How am I supposed to break through all her baggage? Ken asked himself repeatedly. He knew he loved her, he told her he loved her, and he had done so much to demonstrate his love for her. So how could she feel so safe and secure with him, share her entire world with him in ways he knew was unprecedented because she repeatedly told him, "You're the first guy to ever… blah, blah, blah," regarding one thing he did for her after another. He continued to wonder, Just what is it going to take for her to realize the obvious?

A few days went by, and Ken awoke, as he did most mornings, to find his father downstairs on the sofa, watching television. Something was a little different about today, though. His father was usually sulking, but not today. By that afternoon, he was smiling, and a little animated, as he was watching a preseason football game.

"Who's winning, Dad?" said Ken, just taking a shot hoping he'd get a response from his father.

"The Panthers are winning, Ken!" replied his father. "Did you just see that ninety-yard punt return?"

No freaking way! Ken thought excitedly to himself. Ken knew his father would just randomly blurt stuff out, so he wasn't sure if it was a real response to a question or just a coincidence that he asked about something with which a random response just seemed to fit. So, he repeated himself, "Sorry, Dad, who did you say was winning?" He asked again with a desperate tone in his voice, "Dad! Sorry! I didn't quite hear you. Who did you say was winning?"

After a few moments of silence, his dad said, "I could watch that replay all day. One heck of a run."

Ken still couldn't bring himself to be certain if he'd gotten through to his father for a moment or if it was just a random coincidence. He spent a couple of hours within earshot of his father, hoping to gain more insight, but other than his father not sulking and being a little more animated, not much had changed. Ken decided he would take what he could get and be happy about it, much like his attitude toward his relationship with Amy at the moment.

Ken's mind began to wander in Amy's direction. He hadn't seen her yet today and missed her terribly.

His father finally got up and left. Normally, he left without a word, and most of the time Ken would be out of the room just to come back and find he was gone. But today, as he was walking out the door, he turned around and said, "I know it was just a preseason game and it doesn't count for much, but it meant a lot to me to be able to sit here and watch it with you, Kenny boy. Just seemed like old times. I'm really hoping we can watch more games with each other."

"Sure, Dad," responded Ken, not even knowing if his words

would register with his father. He seemed like he was here in the moment, but was he really?

"Now!" said Ken aloud to an empty house, "there's nothing stopping me from going to visit my woman!"

Ken felt like he was walking on air as he left his house for hers. He made it as far as her garage when she came bursting out the kitchen door, practically running to greet him. She embraced him in such a way that she nearly knocked him over, wrapping herself around him and holding him tighter than she'd even held him before. He put his arms around her and heard her whisper in his ear, "I really do love you too, Ken."

Football Season

Over the next few weeks, things began to change in their relationship. Where Amy had always been open with her words, she also became very open with her body, frequently touching Ken, hugging on Ken, and having sex with Ken. She also began to share other things regularly, like the fact that she missed him when he wasn't around. She began to tell him more often that she loved him. She would tell him he looked good, and that she felt the need to hear his voice.

Then she would always take a step back, and Ken would try to bait her into coming back his way by saying things like, "Maybe you are like Amelia Earhart... and a bit lost... I just don't know if you need to find me or I need to find you."

Amy would typically just glare at him for making such statements and never seemed to be baited back to him but had to find her own way back each time. This never deterred Ken from retreating to his Lucy comments, so he went there again with, "Please wake up and come back to me, Lucy."

The Lucy comments had become a bit of game for Ken, giving him a way to vent his frustrations without being confrontational. Then one day she came to him and said, "The more time that goes by, I want us a little more every day." And not long after that, she told him that she felt she was done pulling back, and Ken could see a drastic change in her, as she began to put real effort into remaining in the moment with him.

Ken loved the new level of the relationship but felt himself holding back out of fear that she would retreat again at some point. He openly told her that he wanted to work toward a marriage someday because he was confident he wanted to spend the rest of his life with her, but the most important thing to him was that they worked together to build a healthy relationship. He knew they both screwed up previous marriages, and he wanted her to know that he was willing to put work into this relationship and try to do it right, for both their sakes.

Over the next few months, as they grew closer, it really seemed as though the two of them somehow operated on the same frequency, like they each instinctively knew to pick up where the other left off. Ken automatically knew if Amy wasn't doing well and worked to make her feel better, and Amy was the same way with Ken. If she noticed he was having a bad day, she worked to cheer him up. It was as though they felt each other's joy and pain in the most intimate ways possible. It was uncanny, joyful, and even frightening, all at the same time.

Ken thought maybe this unusual connection was part of what had been difficult for Amy to deal with. As great as it was, you would have to be diving off a cliff into a very serious relationship of trust to build what they had built. Ken knew that Amy had serious trust issues and perhaps finding herself giving in and trusting over and over again when she said she would never, had been a very difficult step for her take.

But things went oddly beyond them just reading each other like open books. One night, Ken dreamt that he was on an airplane and landing at the local airport only to have Amy tell him the next morning that she had dreamt that she needed to pick him up at the airport. These sorts of incidents where they were separate yet seemed entwined with the other became more and more frequent.

Things also seemed to change with Ken's father, especially during the Sunday visits while a game was on. Even when a game wasn't on, his father seemed happier than he had in a long time, but there was still a disturbing verbal disconnect.

"Hi there, Kenny boy!" his father would now frequently say when he entered his home. On Sundays it would generally be, "Are you ready to watch the game, Kenny boy?" or "Do you think we can pull off a win this week, Kenny boy?"

The odd thing for Ken, was that no one had ever called him "Kenny" or "Kenny boy" other than his mother, and those were always her primary go-to names for him. He couldn't recall his mother ever calling him "Ken" and only referring to him as "Kenneth" if she was introducing him to someone, like at church, or the market, or pretty much anywhere, and even though she always called him "Kenny" or "Kenny Boy" she never introduced him that way. It was as if that was her territory, her special name for her son, and no one else was entitled to use it.

His father had never used his mother's nickname for him before. So why now?

Amy began to spend more and more time at Ken's home, spending the night occasionally and always showing up on Sunday. Even though she didn't particularly care for football, she wanted to support Ken in dealing with his father. It hurt each of them a little to see his father like this and hurt each of them a little that he rarely seemed to acknowledge Ken and never once acknowledged Amy's existence. They each felt it best that they did not take it personally, but Ken was determined to get through to his father one way or another.

Finally, Thanksgiving rolled around, and two people couldn't possibly be closer to one another as Amy and Ken. Amy even said, "We can talk about anything. We don't even actually have to talk to know exactly how the other is feeling."

It was true, the two of them were connected verbally, emotionally, and physically, and neither of them felt they could imagine life without the other, and neither of them cared that no one else was ever around. They were content with each other, but they also didn't mind that Ken's father showed up at Thanksgiving to watch football.

Thanksgiving day, his dad was happier than on normal football days, even though his team, the Panthers, weren't playing. He talked almost excessively throughout the day. A lot of his talk was about football and much of it directed at Ken, talking at him, not to him, or so it seemed.

"I'm getting season tickets for us next year in Charlotte, Kenny boy," said his father. "Doesn't that sound like fun?"

"Sure, Dad," responded Ken in a flat tone that indicated he was uncertain if a response even mattered.

At one point, his father had a somber look which slowly consume his face, and he said, "You know, Ken, it killed me inside to lose your mother…" And he paused.

"Wait!" Ken said forcefully with excitement, holding his hand up in a stop motion toward Amy who was doing nothing but going about her business in the kitchen. "He never talks about Mom, and he's trying to… he's actually trying to."

After a moment, as if gaining his composure, his father continued, "She was my world, and I wasn't sure how I'd ever continue without her. But I kept going… or really tried to keep going for you and your sister." He paused again.

"Come on, Dad," said Ken, trying to give some real encouragement. "You're doing good. Give me some more. Tell me what's going on. Please?"

"I just…" And his father began to lose his composure and tear up and stutter a little. "I just don't think I could actually go on if anything happened to you. It would be the end of me."

"I'm not going anywhere, Dad," replied Ken in a gentle yet concerned voice. "I promise I'm not going anywhere at all. What I need, Dad, is for you to come back to me. Do you understand what I'm saying?"

His father regained his composure and turned his attention right back to the game. Then a few minutes later, he added, "I know this is Thanksgiving and all, and I should be thankful, but what I'm really hopeful for right now… is a Christmas miracle!"

"That's it," Ken said to Amy. "I'm going to go see if I can get Carson to come down here and see my dad."

"Uhhh…" replied Amy. "Did I miss something in our previous conversation where he told you he never leaves his farm and basically told you not to come back?"

"He never told me not to come back," replied Ken.

"Uhhh… no, not directly," said Amy. "But you said that he suggested a little agoraphobia could do you some good. Would that not mean that you need to keep your ass at home and not go trekking up to his farm anymore? That's what it certainly seems like to me, anyway. Besides, he's not the type of doctor that your dad needs."

"You're probably right, in as much as I don't need to go waste my time with him," acknowledged Ken, disappointed that there didn't seem to be a solution.

"Good!" said Amy. "Because there's something I need you for this evening."

Ken just gave a "what's that?" kind of glance in her direction, and she replied, "If you don't mind, my back is a bit dry and I could really use some aloe on it. Would you please take care of that for me this evening?"

"Of course, I don't mind," said Ken. "If you have some aloe with you, I'll do it right now."

Amy told him she didn't have any with her, but that he should just come over to her place after his father left, and Ken agreed to do so. A few hours later, Ken walked into Amy's home where she was wearing nothing but a short robe. Ken really didn't think much about it beyond how nice her legs looked.

"Where's the aloe?" Ken asked.

"It's back here," replied Amy, leading him to her bedroom, where she got onto the foot of the bed and squatted on her knees, facing the head of the bed with her back to Ken, who stepped up close behind her. She handed him the aloe then slowly dropped her robe from her body, leaving all exposed.

Ken could feel his heart racing as he emptied some aloe into his hands and began to gently rub her back. It didn't take long before things got heated and the two were engaged in sex, first on her bed, then across a large chair in her room.

When the encounter was finally finished, Ken was getting dressed and Amy was putting her robe back on, when something occurred to Ken and he asked, "You played me?"

"What?" asked Amy with an innocent look on her face, then she turned to quickly exit her room and run down the hallway toward her kitchen.

"You totally played me!" said Ken, chasing her down the hallway and cornering her in the kitchen. "Admit it! You played me!"

"Are you complaining?" she asked.

"Actually, no," laughed Ken. "You can play me like that any time you want!"

The two of them had some wine and enjoyed the rest of their evening, mostly with conversation, with Ken stopping to take care of some things around the house and helping clean up the kitchen, as usual. When Ken finally got ready to leave, late that night, he didn't really feel like he wanted to leave her, and Amy must have felt as though she didn't really want him to leave either, as she said, "Ken... I really do want more."

"What's that?" Ken asked.

"I really do want more with you," said Amy.

Ken smiled and asked, "You're just playing me, again aren't you?"

Amy took that statement seriously and with the straightest possible face she said, "No, I swear, I'm not playing you. I really do want more with you."

Ken said goodnight and walked on out. Where he had felt like he was holding back in this relationship, just expecting her to run again at any moment, he was all-in now. He finally felt that she wanted exactly what he did and felt he could now drop his guard and fully embrace it.

6

Whispers

Amy would regularly go over to Ken's, have sex, then go home, but occasionally she would spend the night. She had told Ken how her second husband snored to the point she had difficulty sleeping and he had always told her it was her problem, not his. Ken knew he snored, but didn't want to be an inconsiderate bastard, like her second husband, so he made a deal with Amy early on that if his snoring ever kept her from sleeping, just to wake him up and he'd go to another room. As much as he wanted to lie beside her, he wasn't about to put her through sleepless nights. Amy did just that, and each time she stayed over, Ken would awake, feeling her gently shaking him in the middle of the night, and all she would have to say is, "you're snoring," and he'd immediately, and without fuss, get up and go to the guest room.

Last night had been a little different, as Ken awoke around 3 am to Amy tossing and turning. He assumed that he had disturbed her, so he got himself up and went to the guest room. Ken awoke again, a little after 6 am, and went back to his bedroom and laid down beside Amy.

"Where did you go?" she asked, sounding like a cross between sleepy and a little angry.

Ken replied, "I woke up about three, and you were tossing and turning, so I figured my snoring must have bothered you, so

I got up and went to the guest room."

"Don't ever do that again," lectured Amy with a stern tone, and she rolled over to go back to sleep.

Ken smiled and rubbed her back for a couple minutes, then she pushed herself up close to him and pulled his arm around her, giving him no choice but to hold her close. The two of them were very content in this moment, each feeling like they belonged to the other as they faded off to sleep again.

Nearly thirty minutes passed, and Ken awoke to a sharp pain in his arm, saying "What the hell?" just loud enough to disturb Amy.

"What is it?" she asked, trying to wake up and focus.

"I don't know," replied Ken, "just had a sharp pain in my arm."

"Left, or right?" asked Amy.

"Right," replied Ken. "Why?"

"Well, if it were a sharp pain in the left arm, then we might have to worry about a heart attack or something," she said with a smile, as she was attempting to make light of something to make him feel better, like she often did with things.

"No," he said, with a serious and curious tone. "It's not like that. It was almost like a bee sting."

"Well, that's just weird," replied Amy, shrugging her shoulders and making a face which showed she was at a loss of words beyond that.

It was an odd sensation, and Ken kept feeling as though he had just been stung, complete with a bit of throbbing in his lower right arm, yet there was nothing visible.

Amy got dressed and left for her house, saying, "Goodbye, Mr. Wilson!" to Ken's father who was sitting on the sofa, watching television as always. She didn't expect a response from him and got exactly that, no response.

Ken got back to work on a set of architectural plans that he was getting eager to finish. Much of the day went by with Ken forgetting about the stinging he had felt that morning, but late in the day, he noticed his arms felt wet, as if they were sweating. Then, he realized, it wasn't just his arms, but he was feeling wet and sweaty all over. The temperature in the house was comfortable, so he didn't understand how he could be sweating. He was determined to continue with his day and try not to focus on it, and after fifteen minutes, it passed.

Ken spent the evening with Amy, as usual, but didn't mention his sweating incident because it now seemed trivial and unimportant. They just shared more of their lives, their triumphs, their pains, and their dreams.

Amy didn't spend the night this time, and Ken awoke alone in his bed early the next morning to another stinging pain in his right arm. It was exactly how it had been the previous morning and at nearly the same time of day. Ken began to worry that something was wrong with himself.

This day continued much like the day before with Ken focused on work, and with no other strange incidents until late in the day when he walked into his living room, where his father was sitting on the sofa watching television. Ken was walking across the room when he stopped cold. He was certain he had just heard whispering, and he looked at his father whose demeanor remained unchanged.

"Why did I expect anything else?" asked Ken aloud to himself. His father never reacted to actual people saying actual things, so why should he expect him to act any differently to "whispers" that he, himself, had likely just imagined. Maybe it was something on the television, he thought, but a few moments later he heard the whispering again. Ken retreated to his bedroom, hoping it was just something on the television and that he wasn't somehow losing his mind.

He sat on the end of his bed, waiting, and hoping not to hear it again. It was just the TV, he kept telling himself. A few moments passed and Ken could feel himself relaxing as he laid back in his bed and closed his eyes. He felt as though he could let himself drift off to sleep, but in the moment between consciousness and sleep, he heard the whispers again. His eyes flew open, and this time it was not only louder, but distinctly multiple voices doing the whispering. Ken sat up and looked around the room. He saw nothing but continued to hear the whispers. Even though they were louder, he couldn't quite make out if something was being said or if it was perhaps some other noise that sounded like whispers.

As much as Ken was trying to rationalize that there had to be some logical explanation, the fact was that this was totally creeping him out. He jumped to his feet, raced downstairs, out his front door, and walked straight over to Amy's. Even though he was half afraid she would think he'd lost his mind, he told her what had just happened to him, and she immediately became concerned for his wellbeing.

Amy did what she could to comfort Ken without patronizing. She affirmed to him that there had to be some logical explanation and then she offered to go over and see if she could hear anything that could help explain what was going on. Ken liked the idea of having a second set of ears and Amy would likely help him pinpoint the source. Or, if he were to hear it and she didn't, then he would at least know it was all in his head, as uncomforting as that thought was.

They sat in Ken's house, in silence, for nearly an hour, with both listening intently for anything that sounded like whispers but heard nothing until Ken's father broke the silence by blurting out, "What the hell?!? Do you believe that?" apparently in response to something on television. Ken and Amy looked at each other and busted out laughing.

"This is ridiculous," said Ken, smiling. "I can't believe we're sitting here, quiet like this, just waiting to confirm if I'm crazy or not. We're never quiet. We always talk… well, at least, you always talk."

Amy gave him a playful kick to his leg, "What do you mean, I always talk? You say plenty when we're together too, mister."

The two of them decided that they would just go about their day and try to act normal. If the whispering returned, then they would deal with it when it happened, but not dwell on it or try to expect it. Amy put on a happy face, but was really worried about her best friend, and planned to stay the night to make sure he was okay.

For the rest of the evening, neither of them heard anything that remotely resembled whispers and they had a good, enjoyable, and normal evening and night together. They got into bed, Amy snuggled up next to Ken, and said, "I love you. I know I don't say it much, but I really do."

"It's okay," replied Ken. "I know you do whether you say it or not. I feel it, and that's what counts… and of course, I love you too."

"Whatever," she replied, rolling her eyes.

Ken felt an overwhelming sense of comfort in how Amy was

there for him, almost like she was trying to watch out for him and do what she could to make him okay. Ken knew he loved her, but more than that he felt great appreciation for her. He had never felt like he needed someone before, but now, he couldn't even imagine his life without her. As awkward as some things had been throughout the development of this relationship, there was nothing that had happened that didn't make it all worthwhile for him. He thought of themselves as being two sides of the same coin, being so much alike, so close, and so inseparable.

Ken laid awake for a couple of hours, going over all that had happened between the two of them, and thinking how lucky he was to have her in his life. Problems like he was having with his father, and hearing the whispers was all so manageable for him, having her in his life. He just knew that everything would always be okay as long as they were together, and as he drifted off to sleep, he realized just how lost he had been his entire life, compared to how he now felt.

The following morning, at about the same time as the previous two mornings, Ken awoke to another sharp sting in his right arm, but this time he saw something.

"Holy shit!" shouted Ken, loudly, and awaking Amy, as he scrambled with everything he had, practically back-peddling in bed, shoving his back into his headboard and reaching for Amy, all at the same time.

He heard the whispers, louder than ever. Amy spun around, completely startled, not as much by Ken's movement in bed, but more because she heard the whispers as well. As unnerving as the whispers were, it prepared neither of them for what they both saw at their bedside.

"My God, Amy!" said Ken. "My God! Please tell me you see

this!"

Amy had her mouth open but was speechless at the sight of what they could only describe as a ghostly figure, standing beside the bed. It was like a misty blue color and had enough definition where they could tell it was a heavyset woman. The apparition was also distinct enough that they could make out facial expressions, and it looked to both of them like she was trying to say something.

Ken stared at the ghostly mouth for a moment, trying to figure out if the movements coincided with any of the whispers, but his biggest problem was that he could hardly make out any words in what seemed like multiple voices whispering.

Not Long for This World

Ken and Amy grabbed some clothes and raced downstairs, with clothing in hand, waiting to get dressed until they felt they had safely escaped the apparition in the bedroom. Ken's father was downstairs when Ken and Amy came running into the room half-naked. "Well…" said Ken slyly, "not to make light of this whole situation, but if there was anything that might get my dad's attention…" And he looked up and down, taking in all the beauty he found in Amy's body.

"You're awful," she replied, tugging on some spandex pants. Then she got serious, and said with a bit of panic in her voice, "What the hell was that? And, what are we supposed to do?"

"Call Ghostbusters?" Ken said, attempting to lighten things up and make her feel a little less scared, but he could see by her expression that it didn't help at all. "You just stay right here for a minute while I go back up and check it out, okay?"

She shook her head slowly, back and forth.

"I take it you don't like that idea?" asked Ken.

"I just don't know what I like the least," said Amy. "You going back up there, or me being left down here alone… because, let's face it, your dad doesn't really count in this situation."

"So, what do you want to do?" asked Ken, trying to put forth a calm demeanor.

"I don't know," replied Amy with a bit of stress in her voice. "Believe it or not, I've never actually been in a situation like this." There was a long pause before she continued, "But I suppose WE need to go up and just see if it's still there."

Before they could build up the courage to take on the flight of stairs, they began to hear the whispers again, and they seemed slightly louder than before. They each looked around, as though they were trying to pinpoint a source for something that seemed to surround them. Ken's father got up from the sofa and began walking directly toward Ken and Amy, and they found that almost as disturbing as the whispering.

"Everything is going to be alright, Kenny boy," said his father as he reached out and placed his hand on Ken's shoulder, then repeated himself, "Everything is going to be alright, my son."

Right as Ken's father was repeating his comforting statement, the heavyset female ghost reappeared beside them. Ken's father was undeterred as both Ken and Amy just about jumped out of their skins, retreating rapidly.

"My house?" asked Amy, in a panicked voice.

"What about my dad?" asked Ken. "I don't want to just leave him. He just acknowledged my existence. Did you see that? Whatever else is going on, I think he may be coming around. He was actually speaking to me and not at me."

"I noticed, and honestly, that's even freaked me out right now," said Amy, clenching his hand in hers. "But he seems undeterred by it... her... whatever it is. Can we at least go outside to have this conversation?"

The ghostly figure turned and began moving toward them, and without speaking another word, the couple made a move for the front door. As they walked out the door, watching behind them, the apparition slowly faded out of existence. Ken started to walk back inside, when Amy grabbed his arm to stop him.

"Do you think it's safe?" asked Amy, whispering, as though she was afraid that it might hear her.

"My dad?" replied Ken, opening his eyes wide at her, like he was stating an obvious problem.

Amy, not letting go of the grip she had on his arm, began walking back into the house with him. The two walked about a dozen paces into the home, then just stopped and looked around.

"I really want to go to my house, right now," said Amy, barely above a whisper. "But I'm not about to leave you and your dad if you really want to stay here."

Ken's father had returned to his spot on the sofa, focused once again, on the television. "Yes," said Ken, "let's go to your place."

The couple, again, walked out of Ken's home, but before they got to Amy's, Ken suggested they walk up to the farm to visit with Carson.

"Why?" asked Amy, with a high level of frustration in her voice. "What do you think he can possibly do?"

"I don't know," replied Ken, "but something he said last time I was up there just stands out in my mind. It's probably nothing. I just have this feeling that he knows things that he's not entirely being honest about. I know that sounds weird…"

"Doesn't sound any weirder than what's been happening today," said Amy. "I'll walk up there with you… especially since I have no desire to be left alone right now."

As the couple began walking through the neighborhood, heading toward the farm, they speculated a bit about what could be going on, but then their conversations began to turn more toward other things and they each found themselves comforted by the sense of normalcy in walking and talking. As they crossed the small bridge over the stream, their conversations turned back to the day's events, the whispers they heard, and the ghost they had seen, wondering how they would sound when explaining it to Carson.

"Is this really a good idea?" asked Amy.

"Afraid he'll think we're crazy?" asked Ken.

Amy laughed, and said, "Maybe... a little."

"Carson either knows something, or he's a bit crazy himself," said Ken, "and I'm at a loss as to what else to do at the moment."

As they walked into the meadow, Amy's personality completely changed again. Just as before, she started talking about things that made little or no sense. She was talking about being independent and not relying on anyone and talking about selling all her belongings and moving away. Ken wasn't certain he could handle her turning squirrelly right now, on top of everything else that was going on. He attempted to talk rationally to her, but he couldn't tell if she didn't hear what he was saying or didn't want to hear. Whatever was up with her, he decided it best to just agree with her irrational statements rather than fight her on them.

As they approached the farmhouse, Carson was sitting right where they left him.

"Does he ever move from that spot or do anything else besides sit there?" Ken wondered aloud, then smiled his best fake smile, and gave a wave to Carson.

They could tell by the curious look on Carson's face that he was wondering what the purpose of their visit was, so they got right to the point. They told him about Ken's sharp arm pains, thinking it must be related, somehow, since the last time it happened, the whispering and ghost coincided with it. Then it began to trouble Amy that Carson didn't react as though there was anything abnormal about what they were telling him. In fact, he barely reacted at all, as it seemed like he was contemplating more on what he wanted to say in response.

"So why come to me with this?" asked Carson.

"Because of something you asked me, the last time I was up here," replied Ken.

"That was quite some time ago," replied Carson. "You'll have to refresh my memory."

"When I talked to you about Amy being sick, you asked if she was experiencing any hallucinations," explained Ken.

"That's quite a leap to the two of you sharing a hallucination, don't you think?" asked Carson.

"Told you we were wasting our time coming up here," blurted Amy, who was now also feeling that Carson knew something but was holding back.

Carson just sat there for a moment, looking at the two of them, then he turned his focus to Ken, and said, "You are not long for this world my friend, and that's about all I can say."

"Amy," said Ken sternly, in a way he had never spoken to her before, "please start walking toward the meadow and give me a moment with Dr. Matthews."

Amy briefly looked at Ken with an "are you serious" kind of look, then she got up and walked off the porch and headed for the meadow. Ken waited until she was out of earshot, then asked Carson, "Just what the hell do you think you're doing?"

"Being as honest as I can be at the moment," replied Carson.

"You're just scaring her," said Ken on the verge of anger. "And I won't have that."

"She needs to be a little scared," said Carson, calmly and with a smile, letting Ken know that his anger didn't faze him.

"You know something about this," said Ken. "I know you do. But you're not going to help us, are you?" And, with that, Ken got up to leave.

As Ken was walking off the porch, Carson asked, "Do you love that woman? I mean, really love that woman?"

"Of course," said Ken without hesitation, and turned to face Carson.

"Then this is all you need to know..." said Carson. "You can hang onto that love all you want, and it might be enough, but I doubt it. I'll say it again, you are not long for this world, and the best thing you can do is prepare her for your departure."

Ken just looked aghast.

"Please, for her sake," continued Carson, "tell her she should come up here for safety if anything should happen to you. And, I will make you this promise... if you ever make it back up here to see me, then I will tell you anything you want to know. I'm afraid, that's the best I can do right now."

Ken, feeling truly puzzled by Carson's words, gave a half-hearted wave goodbye and walked off to join Amy, where she was dancing around in the meadow. Ken grabbed Amy's hand, and she continued her odd behavior until they crossed the bridge, then the couple walked through the neighborhood and back home in silence.

As they walked up to Ken's front door, Amy was back to her normal self and couldn't bite her tongue any longer. "Well, are you going to tell me what he said? What was that nonsense about you not being long for this world? What they hell was that supposed to mean?"

Before Ken could answer anything, Amy added, "And now I think I'm more afraid than before we went up there. And we're sleeping at my place tonight, and I won't hear you say anything otherwise."

"Yes ma'am," said Ken. "And as far as Carson goes, just don't think anything else of it, okay?"

They slept at Amy's that night and both tossed and turned a great deal. Ken awoke much earlier than normal the next morning and couldn't get back to sleep. As he was getting up, Amy awoke, asking where he was going and if he could come back to bed.

"I can't sleep anymore," said Ken. "And I want to be at my place when Dad arrives this morning."

"Then I'm getting up and going with you," demanded Amy.

The two of them were standing in Ken's kitchen when his front door opened and there was his dad, standing in the doorway, but this time he was not alone. After a moment, his dad closed the front door and walked on in by himself.

"What they heck?" asked Ken. "Dad! Was that Janice?"

His father just walked over to the sofa as if he didn't hear the question and sat down.

"That was Janice," Ken said to Amy, and heading for his front door.

"Your sister?" Amy asked, knowing he had talked about her before, but uncertain if that was exactly who he was referring to.

"Yes," replied Ken, now at his front door, opening it to look for his sister, but she wasn't there.

Amy had not seen her, so she asked, "Are you sure it was

her?"

"Yes," said Ken, somewhat uncertainly. "Or at least I think it was."

It was now about the same time as the previous mornings when Ken felt the bee sting sensation, as he let out a, "Dammit…" followed by a reluctant, "Oh no… not again."

The whispers began, louder than ever, and Amy began to tremble in fear. The female ghost appeared again but wasn't alone this time as there were two other ghosts with her, a thin female and a young man.

"I'm not feeling so well," gasped Ken, as he fell to his knees.

Amy tried grabbing ahold of him and went to the floor with him. Ken's father got up from the sofa, walked over and stood over the couple, as Ken's front door opened, and Janice walked in.

"I'm really not feeling well!" Ken cried out.

Amy kept trying to comfort him, cradling him in her arms as she was now sitting on the floor with Ken's head in her lap, and she just kept repeating, "You'll be okay."

"I don't think so," said Ken, with his father, sister, and three apparitions now standing around them. "Please go back to the farmhouse if anything happens to me."

"Nothing is going to happen to you," said Amy, weeping.

"Promise me," said Ken.

"I promise," replied Amy, adding, "But nothing is going to happen to you."

The front door opened again, and the whispers turned into a full-blown chaos of voices.

"Wendy?" said Ken, with tears streaming down his face.

Amy recognized the name, Wendy, as being Ken's daughter,

but she didn't see anyone there.

"Ken, please hang on," begged Amy, so focused on him that she no longer cared about the ghosts or voices. "Please, please, please hang on."

It didn't matter how much she begged. Ken was gone.

The Awakening

There are few things that people tend to gather for outside of the holidays, and mostly its weddings and funerals. Theodore (Ted) Wilson, Ken's father, had been driven today by Ken's sister, Janice, who walked Ted Wilson to the door, before turning to go back for her cellphone she had forgotten in her car. A few other close family and friends soon gathered outside. Most made small talk, uncertain of what to say about what was going on. For most, it had been two years since they had even seen Ken.

Wendy, Ken's twenty-one-year-old, fair-haired daughter, arrived just in time, but was afraid to walk in. She had been very close to her father and had done everything she could to avoid seeing him like this. Her father had always been big, strong, and indestructible in her eyes. This had all been more than she could bear, but she took a deep breath, told herself she would be strong, and walked through the door.

Wendy made her way through the crowded room to her father, and just as she did, Ken's eyes opened wide.

"I need everyone to back up," said the heavy-set nurse who had been in regularly each morning to change out Ken's I.V.

"One familiar person can stay close," said a thin, female doctor.

"I'll stay close," said Ted Wilson, and a young male orderly stepped out of his way to allow him better access to his son.

Ken's face was riddled with confusion, and he desperately wanted to speak, but he couldn't get any words to come out of his mouth.

"He's trying to say something," said Ted Wilson.

"As soon as he calms down, we'll give him some ice chips," said the nurse, "but it will be awhile before he can use those vocal cords again."

Ken's father had his hand on Ken's shoulder, trying to calm him down, and explained, "So glad to have you back with us, Kenny boy, you've given us all quite a scare, but you're going to be okay. You've just been in a coma for a while. You had a feeding tube in your throat for a long time, so don't even try to talk just yet."

Ken looked panicked and confused, and when he realized he could not speak no matter how hard he tried, he began trying to make a motion as though he wanted to write something, but he was so weak, that he wasn't sure they were understanding him, and he wasn't sure he could even write, as his hand was severely trembling with him just trying to find the strength to raise it.

"Did you bring your iPad with you, Wendy?" asked Ted. "I think he wants to write something."

Wendy stepped forward and presented her iPad to her grandfather, set up and ready to go for her father to scribble with his finger. Ted took the pad and attempted to hold it steady for his son. It was difficult for Ken, he was shaky, and it looked like the writing of a four-year-old, but they could all make out exactly what he wrote, although none of them knew what it meant, as he simply wrote, "Amy?"

"Amy?" several of them said at once, then they all began looking at each other with the same question in mind: Who is

Amy?

Ken was visibly frustrated, and Ted held the pad close to his son's hand again. Ken kept poking at what he had written, until his sister Janice said, "Ken, none of us understand. Who is Amy?"

Ken began crying and kept poking at the screen for a few more moments, then he began to scribble again, sloppily adding, "Where is" above "Amy?"

They all began speculating on who Amy could be. They asked Wendy, "Did your father have a girlfriend we didn't know about?"

Wendy, looking as clueless as the rest of them replied, "Not that I know of. I don't know of anyone he knew named Amy."

"Janice," said Ted, "some of the folks he works with are out in the waiting room, can you please go see if they know who Amy is?"

Janice walked out to the waiting room and questioned everyone. They were all thrilled that Ken had come completely out of the coma, as expected this morning, but none of them knew who Amy could be. By the time Janice reported back to the room, Ken was as out-of-control as a newly awakened coma patient could be, and the doctor felt it best to sedate him for now.

The family and friends who had showed up quickly cycled through the room, trying to show their support. They all wanted Ken to know they would be there for him in any way they could, but Ken quickly fell asleep because of the sedative, so everyone just tried to give words of comfort and support to the immediate family before departing. Ted, Janice, and Wendy were all who remained in the room after a few minutes.

Ken slept most of the day, and when he awakened, it was a

repeat of before. All he seemed to care about was Amy, and he seemed very agitated that no one could give him an answer. When they explained to him he had been in a coma for nearly two years, he just shook his head as though he didn't believe it. It didn't take long before he got himself so worked up, that he had to be, again, sedated.

Ted, Janice, and Wendy decided they would take shifts as night began to fall. Janice gave Ted her car keys and insisted on being the one to stay the night since her father had spent so much of his time there over the past couple of years.

Around 2 am, Janice awoke to Ken making some grunting sounds. He wanted to write again, but Janice wouldn't give him the iPad, and said, "You just want to ask about Amy again, don't you?"

Ken nodded, with tears in his eyes.

"Ken," said Janice softly, "I can tell that whoever Amy is, she must mean a whole lot to you, but if you keep getting worked up, and they keep having to sedate you, then you are just dragging things out. You must remain calm, then get yourself better, so you can talk and move. Then, we can talk about Amy as much as you like. Okay?"

Ken shook his head and looked very sad. Janice could tell he didn't like what she was saying, but he was slowly accepting it, anyway. She sat up with him for the next two hours, explaining that he had been in a horrible car accident and had been in a coma for nearly two years. She then tried to fill him in on all he had missed in the world, everything she could think of from movies and music, to what his daughter had been up to in college and the boy that had just broken her heart. Ken listened intently to Janice, mostly in disbelief, and then he nodded as if to show that was enough for now and fell off to sleep.

The next morning, they moved Ken to a different room in the hospital and began his rehabilitation which lasted about three weeks. To Ken, he was just going through motions, not excited about anything, and very little would occupy his mind, other than Amy. He quickly learned to keep most of it to himself, only confiding in Janice about how much he missed her.

Janice listened and indulged him as much as she could throughout the rest of his hospital stay. She desperately wanted to tell him that none of it was real, that it was only a dream, but she could see how bad he already hurt, and she didn't want to be the one to crush his world. She would listen to him go on and on about Amy, tearing up each time, at a minimum, then fall into full-blown sobs at other times. Ken shared with Janice about how much Amy had changed his life, and how he finally felt something for someone.

One afternoon, Ken began wailing loudly, and crying out Amy's name. He was so loud that two nurses came running into his hospital room, questioning what was going on. None of the family could answer what triggered Ken, but the television was on, and the movie 50 First Dates was playing. No one could get him to calm down enough so they could understand what was wrong, so they sedated him.

Janice knew her brother had always been the loner type. Growing up, everyone always made fun of Ken because he didn't like people to touch him. He didn't like to hug anyone. She had never once heard him admit he loved anyone, but here he was professing love for a woman in a dream. It was one of the saddest things she had ever seen. At one point, Ken even sent a group text to the family telling them all how much he appreciated and loved them. This was so out of character that Ken's daughter rushed to hospital because she was certain that he must be dying. Ken had definitely changed, and as sad as it was to watch him missing Amy, some changes in him were for the better.

Janice remained at a total loss of how anyone could become so attached to someone that didn't even exist. She tried talking to the young female doctor who was assigned to his case, but if he didn't seem in danger of harming himself out of depression, she believed it would eventually pass and he would be okay. But, most of the people in Ken's life, seeing how depressed he was, were fearful that he could be suicidal, even though Ken kept insisting that he wasn't, that he had to remain alive in order to find Amy again.

Janice was a realtor, and other than occasionally having to show a home, she was taking a leave of absence from work so she could keep a close eye on her brother. She had already moved plenty of her stuff into the guest room at Ken's home, where she was determined to see him through all of this and help him back to a normal life.

They finally discharged Ken from the hospital, and they placed him in a wheelchair and rolled him down to Janice's car. After nearly two years, he would finally get to go home, but Ken wasn't the slightest bit excited about it. He continued to be down and depressed at the loss of Amy in his life, despite the efforts of all to cheer him up.

He made it clear to Janice that he would be okay with her being in his home for a while to help and keep him company, but also made it clear that she was to keep everyone besides their dad and Wendy away. He had no desire to see anyone, as he didn't want to have to pretend to be happy, and he didn't want to have to field anymore questions regarding suicide.

Dealing with people had become very uncomfortable for Ken from the standpoint that every conversation always went in the same direction. People would tell him he should be happy he survived the car accident and the coma and how grateful he should be that he'd gotten a second chance. Then, after a few minutes, they would see how depressed he was, then he would watch them tiptoe around the subject of suicide. Where a few people came out and asked directly, most would say things like, "I had this friend that got really depressed… and we didn't think anything about it, then one day he shot himself… so I'm just worried…" or "you wouldn't hurt yourself or anything like that would you?" or his favorite, "you're not thinking of doing anything… stupid… are you?"

Often, he wanted to reply, "Stupid? You think it would be stupid to relieve myself of unbearable pain? Huh? You enjoy seeing me in pain that much that you want to keep me around so you can see more of it?" But he knew better than to let things like that come out of his mouth or he would end up locked up in a room on suicide watch, so he just told everyone exactly what they needed to hear: "I'm fine."

Wendy and Ted helped Janice get Ken and his belongings into her car, then Wendy rolled the wheelchair back into the hospital, and Ted walked off to his own car in the parking lot.

"Was it real?" Ken asked himself for the first time, regarding Amy, as Janice drove the car away from the hospital.

It Wasn't Real

Janice pulled into Ken's driveway, and Ken just sat for a moment, staring at the same house he'd spent much of the last two years in, with Amy, in the same neighborhood, with Amy's house right next door. He began to weep, missing her so much. Then he wiped his eyes and stared hard at Amy's house for a moment, before getting out of the car and walking next door, with his legs still a bit wobbly from lack of use for two years.

"Ken?" Janice called out, holding onto a duffle bag of Ken's that she had just removed from the car. "Where are you going, Ken?"

He made a beeline for the neighbor's front door. Janice dropped the bag and went after him, but before she could stop him, he opened the door and walked in as though it were his place. It quite startled the older couple inside at the stranger entering their home, with the man of the house saying in a shaky voice, "Can we help you?"

Janice came in right as the man was questioning Ken, and tried to neutralize the situation, telling them it was okay, that he just had gotten out of the hospital and was a little confused. Janice began apologizing profusely, all while Ken dropped to his knees and began sobbing in the middle of their living room.

Janice was trying to lift Ken back to his feet and the older man walked over and began helping her get him up and out of their house. Once outside, Ken began walking back to the car, and he was crying so hard, that his words were barely audible as he said, "Can you please drive me around the neighborhood?"

Janice agreed and drove Ken around the thriving neighborhood where people were out working on their lawns, children were out playing, and people were walking down the sidewalks. When they got to the backside of the neighborhood, Ken got out of the car to see there was a stream, but no footbridge to cross it, and there was no farm on the other side. Janice hopped out right behind him.

"It wasn't real," sobbed Ken. "It wasn't real, it wasn't real, it wasn't real… which means… Amy wasn't real. None of it was real. I just can't believe it."

Janice began rubbing her brother's back, attempting to comfort him, and said, "No, Ken, it wasn't real. I'm so sorry. I know you want her to be real, and you want your relationship to be real. From all that you've told me, she sounds like she was perfect for you, but she's not actually here. I'm sorry. Let's get you home, okay?"

Once Janice got Ken settled into his home, she tried again to comfort him by saying, "I don't know that you should look at Amy or any of that experience as not being real since it was all very real to you."

Ken gave her a curious look, and she continued, "Why not look at it all as a positive experience that just came to an end… for whatever reason. The rest of us have been lamenting over poor Ken for two years because you've been in a coma. But, somehow, you came out of it a more loving person. You are more open and accepting of affection than I've… than anyone has ever seen you be. Granted, you're severely depressed and we've got to work through that, but your attitude toward your family is much better. I once read somewhere that our brain helps train us during sleep by giving us scenarios to prepare us in real life. Maybe, just maybe, your subconscious created a world you needed to make you a better person. Despite what happened to you in those two years, the outcome, the growth you've experienced as a person, is very real."

"I don't know," replied Ken. "It doesn't seem to matter how I think about Amy… I don't just miss her; I ache for her… all day… every day. Every time I think about how much I just want to hold her, I can't help it… I start tearing up."

For weeks, Ken remained depressed over the loss of Amy in his life. He was withdrawn and continued to avoid most everyone in his life. He knew that no one wanted to hear about Amy, but there was nothing else he wanted to think about or talk about. He would sit at his drafting table for hours to produce little to no work. He was non-functional, and this had his immediate family getting more worried by the day. They all thought it would get easier for him, but it didn't. Even Ken believed it would get easier eventually, but it wasn't. For him, there seemed to be no end to the agony he felt in missing Amy, no matter how much he told himself that none of it was real.

The weeks turned into months, and at least once a day, Janice would hear the haunting sound of her brother wailing throughout the house. He would cry out her name, sometimes over and over, out of sheer helplessness to change the situation.

"Amy, Amy, please come back to me!" he was wailing loudly. "Dear God, please! Please! Bring her back to me!"

Janice began to break down and cry regularly. Her crying was also a feeling of helplessness to do anything for her brother.

She had encountered no one so sad and pathetic over the loss of another and was clueless what to do for him, other than recommend therapy, which she often did.

Ken would ignore the suggestions for therapy and would typically take it as an opening to talk about Amy, saying things like, "Did I ever tell you how she watched out for me with my sensory issues? She's the only one who ever truly clued in on that, genuinely got it, and watched out for me."

Just how real was this other world he created in his head? Began to question Janice. Seems like too many details and memories for just an ordinary dream. Then she would shake her head and keep thinking to herself, don't let yourself get drawn into his psychosis, Janice.

Ken remained non-functional for five months before Janice, one day, forced him in the car for an outing. "Where are we going?" Ken asked.

Janice didn't even look at him, but replied with a smile, "let's call it a surprise."

When they pulled up to the office building, Ken immediately noticed the signage on the door for Dr. James Tyler. Janice had brought him to a psychiatrist, and she was well prepared to fight Ken on this anyway she had to. He was beginning treatment today, whether he liked it or not, and she already had the backing of the family to get him committed if he completely refused to cooperate. She took a deep breath and prepared for what Ken was about to throw her way.

"Well, what are you waiting for?" asked Ken. "I guess we should head on in and get this over with."

"You mean you aren't going to fight me on this?" asked Janice.

"No… but I want you to go in with me," said Ken. "I don't want to do it alone."

"Okay… as long as that's okay with the doc, I'm good with it," replied Janice.

Dr. Tyler just asked that Janice sit off to the side, out of Ken's line of sight, and observe rather than take part. If she felt she had something she needed to add, then she should raise her hand and when Dr. Tyler thought it appropriate, then he would allow her to weigh in.

"So why are we here today?" Dr. Tyler asked of Ken.

"Because I lost my best friend, my lover, someone who was more like family to me than my own family… and I miss her so much that I can't eat… I can't sleep… and even though I now believe the relationship wasn't real… I still can't stop missing her," answered Ken.

"What do you miss the most about her?" asked Dr. Tyler.

"Her embrace, her smell, her voice…" And Ken began to tear up.

"It is unusual that someone would think they remember a smell from a dream," observed Dr. Tyler. "Why don't you start from the beginning and tell me how you two got together."

Ken told the doctor how he had seen her soon-to-be ex-husband belittling her outside that morning, and then about the lengthy conversation that immediately followed between himself and Amy. He then moved on to their walk through the neighborhood, and the farm they found and boldly walked up to, only to meet this strange character by the name of Dr. Carson Mathews.

Ken kept talking and explaining, even though he noticed what sounded like a gasp behind him. He also noticed that Dr.

Tyler glanced at his sister and put his hand up in a stop motion. Ken figured his sister had come up with something that she felt she needed to say and was raising her hand, but it was nothing of the sort. Janice had gasped, and she was tearing up and hyperventilating.

"OH... MY... GOD!" Janice finally said loudly, unable to hold back any longer, and with her voice cracking.

Dr. Tyler gave her a stern look for being out of place, and Ken's head snapped around rapidly to look at his sister when she uttered the words, "Amelia Earhart."

"Amy is short for Amelia, isn't it?" asked Janice, already certain of the answer.

10

The Cure

"I know that wasn't her exact name," said Janice. "But that's what it reminded me of... wait! It was Amelia Hart! Yeah, that's her, isn't it?"

Ken was stunned and speechless. He had spent months trying to convince himself that none of it was real and he had been desperately trying to come to terms with the fact that he would never see Amy again. The conflict which had been brewing in Ken was incredible because, against what everyone told him and what defied common sense, in his heart, he could not stop believing that he would be with her again.

Janice got up and reached her hand out for Ken's, like she was collecting a child, "Come on, we're going." Then she looked at Dr. Tyler and said, "Sorry, seems I brought him to the wrong doc. We have to go see another."

They walked outside, but before they could get into the car, Ken froze and said, "I think you need to tell me what's going on," and Janice could see he was rapidly becoming emotional.

"I'm so sorry, Ken," said Janice, almost in tears. "I really should have listened to you much closer. I really should have taken what you said more seriously, but I will make this up to you if I possibly can. I just didn't put things together until I just heard you talk about Dr. Carson Mathews."

"What does he matter?" asked Ken.

"We are going to go see another Dr. Mathews," replied Janice. "Dr. Melissa Mathews, the daughter of Carson Mathews. Now get in the car, please."

Melissa Mathews had followed her father's career, working in the same hospital, in the same field, and had been the thin female doctor in the room when Ken awoke from his coma. As Janice began driving for the hospital, she explained how she spent a lot of time in the waiting room down the hall from Ken's room. As a creature of habit, she frequently sat in the same seat, facing the same wall, with a plaque honoring Dr. Carson Mathews. She then explained to Ken that Carson had been in a coma for nearly a decade in a room right across the hall from Ken.

When they arrived at the hospital, which was only a mile down the road from Dr. Adams' office, they went up to the fourteenth floor and asked if Dr. Melissa Mathews was working. They found out she was and had just started her rounds.

"We're heading to room 1432, so perhaps we'll just catch her as she works through," said Janice.

"Room 1432?" asked Ken.

Janice didn't reply, she just grabbed him by the arm and hurried him along down the hall, and into room 1432. Ken entered the room and began to tremble.

"I take it that's her?" asked Janice, watching Ken rush to Amy's side, who was lying in a coma, surrounded by medical equipment, hooked to monitors, and with a feeding tube running down her throat.

"Not in a million years," said Janice. "Not in a million years could I have imagined that you've been locked in a coma and somehow communicating with the other two coma patients on this floor. Dr. Carson Matthews is across the hall, and Amy was in the room right beside yours, the whole time. I'm so sorry I didn't believe she existed."

Ken sat at Amy's bedside, talking to her, and barely paying attention to Janice, or the fact that Amy's mother, Bea Darko, entered the room. Even though Ken had never met Amy's mother, he didn't particularly care for her after hearing all the things Amy had said about her. Ken felt like Amy's biggest issues, especially lack of trust, all stemmed back to how she had been treated, and betrayed, by her own parents. Ken would keep his mouth shut where she was concerned as it wasn't his place, at least not right now, to call her out on the damage she had done to her daughter.

"You look familiar," said Bea to Janice. "Are you a friend of Amy's?"

"Noooo…" replied Janice slowly, trying to figure out just how to explain things. "My brother was in the room next to this one for nearly two years, so I've been on this floor quite a bit."

"Oh!" Bea said, looking confused. "Is that him next to my daughter?" Before Janice could answer, she continued with another question, "And why are you here?"

"It's difficult to explain," replied Janice, observing the woman becoming uncomfortable with their presence.

Dr. Melissa Mathews entered the room, paused, looked around at everyone, smiled, then said, "Am I interrupting something?"

"Just the person I needed to see," said Janice. Then she began to explain how her brother had apparently been communicating with Amy, somehow, while in his coma. She began sharing many of the details of their relationship that Ken had previously shared with her.

Ken got up from Amy's bedside and walked over to stand with Janice, to help confirm what she was saying. Dr. Mathews gave Ken a blank stare, as though she was trying to size him up and choose her words carefully.

"Your dad gave me that same look on a couple of occasions," observed Ken.

"I'm sorry," said Bea, interrupting, "but do you expect me to believe that you've been, somehow, communicating with my daughter, who's been lying here unconscious for nearly two-and-a-half years? I just don't buy it."

"Well, he has," replied Janice.

"I need you all to either prove it or leave," stated Bea.

Ken turned to face Bea, and said, "Your daughter has been married three times. The first was short and you know how all that ended. The second and third were basically two different versions of the same person. Both suffered from little man syndrome, meaning they were both little men who tried to push others around to make themselves feel better. She clearly has a type. She gave up all her possessions for the second, complained about it, then did the same for the third, Adam. Adam turned out to be the biggest ass of them all and her worst mistake ever. Turned out he was just very angry toward women in general because he was a closet homosexual. He just wanted a woman around for show more than anything, using swim meets to pick up random men, any chance he got. He would fabricate most any excuse to explain his bad behavior and cover for who he really was. All the signs were there that he was a total douche, but she ignored the obvious and hitched her wagon to his, anyway. Is that enough detail about your daughter, or would you like for me to go on?"

"That's plenty," replied Bea, with a confused look on her face. "And Adam was a real SOB. I walked into this hospital the morning after the wreck, with her in a coma and him standing over her bed cussing at her as though she were worthless. Did you know that SOB couldn't even be bothered to add her to his health insurance after they were married. Do you know how screwed we are with medical bills because of him? Believe me, my daughter has clearly proven time and time again that she is incapable of making good decisions for herself. Which is why I would question why you, of all people, would take any sort of interest in her, given what her bad decisions did to you."

"What are you talking about?" asked Ken, taking notice of Janice shaking her head.

"You mean you don't know?" asked Bea, looking at Janice. "Just how do you think you ended up in a coma?"

"I was in a car accident," replied Ken.

"Ken," said Janice, softly, "I didn't want you to know anyone else was affected by the accident. I didn't know how you'd take it. I was afraid you might blame yourself. I thought it was enough that you'd been stuck in a coma for two years."

"She drank an entire bottle of wine," said Bea, with an attitude, "then got behind the wheel of a car. You, sir, can blame the miserable two years you had lying in a hospital bed on another one of her bad decisions."

"I think we're way off track," said Janice, turning her attention to Dr. Matthews, "and I think we need to focus on how we put Ken back in touch with Amy, if that's possible. What if he could go back in there… wherever there is… and somehow get to her again?"

They all talked and argued for several minutes. Dr. Matthews listened intently to what Ken had to say about Amy, and Ken wrapped it all up with, "I would boldly walk through the gates of Hell if I needed to do so to get her back, so there is truly nothing I would not do for her, no lengths I would not go to. I know if I can reach her, if I can have one more chance to get through to her, then I can get her on the right path, and hopefully out of her coma and back into her right state of mind. If anyone can do this for her, it's me, and I know it."

"So, can't you guys induce a coma to get him back in?" asked Janice, looking hopefully at the doctor.

"The hospital would never go for it," said Melissa, "especially given what happened to my father. He was placed into an induced coma twice, and the second time, he never came out."

"Yeah," said Ken, "I think he didn't come out because he didn't want to come out. It was over some woman he met in there."

"What was her name?" asked Melissa.

"Anna, I believe," replied Ken. "Why?"

"My father had a shared cognitive theory when it came to coma patients," answered Melissa. "There is so much we don't know about how the mind works. For the most part, we have believed that coma patients don't even dream because we can't see any evidence of brainwaves to prove different, but we've had coma patients wake up and tell us about their dreams. My father believed that those in a coma were on a different plane of existence, and involved, or existed, in something much more than just dreams, where the mind is elevated to a point that it can see outside the body and even connect with others. My mother was in a coma, horseback riding accident, and my father claimed to have connected with her the first time, then induced the second time and never came out. Even though my mother died years ago, he still remains in a coma."

"He has a headstone for her next to his farmhouse," explained Ken, "and he said he could never leave that home because of the memories he has there with her. I'm really sorry."

"The doctor side of me has to tell you no to inducing a coma," said Melissa definitively just before she began tearing up and putting her hand on her heart, "but Melissa's heart has to say yes, that you need to find a way to be there for her, and bring her back if you can."

"Just how big a deal is it to induce a coma?" asked Janice.

Melissa smiled and said, "You probably should have thought that part through prior to asking for it, but… it's not that difficult, just a matter of increasing anesthetic until a monitor shows his brainwaves in the right range. If my father was right, Ken does need to be physically located near Amelia, and lucky for us, the room next door remains empty. I'll get everything we need in the next hour… before I come to my senses and change my mind."

11

The Meaning of Life

Janice and Ken walked into Ken's old hospital room to await Dr. Melissa Matthews, and as soon as they closed the door and had some privacy, Janice said, "Ken, I've actually been a little jealous because you've been painting a picture of the most wonderful relationship I've heard of. I don't know that I have ever known another man who was so devoted to the woman he loves… but… until I heard you speak to Amy's mother, I had no idea she also had so much baggage."

Ken just looked at Janice, cocking his head a bit to one side, knowing there must be something she was trying to get at.

Janice continued, "Even though Dr. Matthews said they can induce a coma, that doesn't mean it's without risk. You heard her say that the second time for her father has kept him in one for ten years. I guess what I'm trying to ask is…if she has issues, and she just ruined the last two years of your life, are you sure this is a woman you really want to be with and risk yourself for?"

"I know she isn't perfect," replied Ken, smiling at the thought of Amy, "but neither am I… or any of us… but she's perfect for me. You know how out of sorts I've always been. When have you ever heard me admit I loved anyone? Never. She has made me a better man in ways that I couldn't have imagined, by bringing out the best in me when I'm with her. I see her imperfections, and I love her despite them. Can you understand that?"

Janice smiled and nodded.

Ken continued, "I've always heard people question the meaning of life, and I really believe I have the answer, or at least I have my answer. There will always be good times and bad times. There will always be happy times and sad times, but what gives all of life meaning is to be able to share it with a mate who is your best friend in the world. Because right now I know my life is pretty meaningless without her."

Janice and Ken weren't in the room long before the doctor, the heavyset nurse, and the male orderly who were attending to Ken when he was a patient, began moving in and out of the room, setting up for the procedure. When all was in place, an anesthesiologist entered the room. Ken got on the bed, laid back, gave a thumbs up, and they started the anesthetic.

"If you see my father again, tell him I'm getting married and I need him to show up to my wedding," said Dr. Matthews.

Ken nodded and just as he felt like he was drifting off, he was immediately out cold. The plan was to give him two hours.

The next thing Ken knew, he was waking up in his home. Something was different, and he wasn't sure what at first, as he walked around his home, touching random objects. Then he realized he was back in and could go find Amy.

I'll start with her place, he thought, as he opened his front door to walk outside, but he wasn't prepared for what he saw. Everything was dark and eerie, as though night had fallen in some ghoulish nightmare of a neighborhood. The only light was from streetlamps, some of which were standing, some were bent, and some were drooped over like the branch of a willow tree.

Most of the homes looked deformed, as though parts of them had melted or vanished altogether.

As disturbing as the landscape was, what struck Ken the most was the darkness. It had not been dark when he left the real world, and he knew he only had two hours. So was it really dark? He wondered. How long was I out? Could I have gotten trapped here?

He went next door and began searching for Amy, but there was no trace of her.

She must be at the farm, he thought, and quickly headed in that direction.

As he approached the stream, he noticed something very odd; like a complete division between night and day, with night on his side of the stream and day on the farm side. He crossed the walking bridge into daylight and began walking uphill to the farmhouse.

As he approached the farmhouse, he could see Carson sitting in his same spot on the porch, but he didn't remain there. When Carson spotted Ken, he jumped to his feet, walked over to the edge of his porch and leaned over his railing.

"You said if I ever made it back, that you'd give me some answers," said Ken as he walked up on the porch and shook Carson's hand.

"I did say something like that, didn't I?" replied Carson with a sly smile. "The answer to your first question is that she is inside the house, probably laying on the sofa... that's where she spends most of her time these days."

Amy had thought she heard voices and walked out onto the porch. Ken noticed she had what looked like a piece of paper in her left hand, and the way it was flopping back and forth, he could tell she was trembling. He walked over to give her a hug, and she hugged him back, but still couldn't bring herself to believe she was really with him again.

"At first, I thought you'd make it back," said Carson, "but then after a while, we began to give up on you."

"Maybe," said Ken, slowly, "if you had been more honest with me, then perhaps I would have been able to figure things out a little quicker."

"That's fair," replied Carson. "But have you ever heard a variation of this old joke; what's the difference between a neurosurgeon and God?"

Ken shook his head, at a loss for an answer.

"God doesn't think that he's a neurosurgeon," answered Carson, "but… you see… in here… we are gods! In here, we can manipulate the hell out of this place and quite literally make it anything we want. We each desired some sort of balance before, but how was I to know that you wouldn't wield your power against me somehow, if you figured out what you guys can do? It was just a simple matter of trust, and I couldn't afford to trust two other gods. The longer you guys remained in the dark, the longer my tranquil, little lifestyle was safe."

"So that's why you gave us the story of Anna just happening to wander up to your farm one day?" asked Ken, "because you couldn't tell us the truth, that she was your wife, and you had yourself induced into a coma so you could be with her?"

"Now, you're getting it," said Carson with a big grin, "but just because you understand what's going on here, doesn't mean you're going to get what you came for. You do know that, right?"

"I don't know," said Ken. "Maybe, maybe not. I am hoping

that for once, you'll be helpful."

"And tell you how to get her out, you mean?" replied Carson. Ken just nodded.

"When you were on your way out before, and I told you that you were not long for this world," said Carson, "I would never have thought it possible for you two to end up in the real world together. But Amy has been stuck in this fantasy world without you for too long. She has missed you so badly, that I think it's made her appreciate what you guys have together. It's made her realize just how much she does love you… and that… might just be enough to get her to wake back up to reality. Might. But this poor gal also keeps cycling through something… I don't know… it's like her entire personality changes and she becomes…"

"Squirrelly?" injected Ken.

"Exactly!" replied Carson. "And when she gets like that, she refuses to listen to reason."

"I'm right here!" Amy said, raising her hand in the air. "I'm literally right here, and you guys are talking as though I'm not."

Both the guys stopped and looked at her.

"I've got nothing to actually add," said Amy meekly. "Just pointing out that I'm here."

"What do you want?" asked Ken, still looking at Amy. "Do you want to remain in this fantasy world or are you willing to come back to reality by fighting for us?"

"I don't know," replied Amy.

"What do you mean you don't know?" asked Ken.

"Look around," said Amy. "This farm and everything around it is beautiful. I get some sense of comfort here, and I kinda love it in a way."

"You do realize," Ken said and paused, "that you love

something that's not real?"

"I guess," answered Amy.

"There is only one shot at this, Amy," said Ken trying to remain calm. "If I can't get you to step out of this fantasy world and into reality, then you're going to be stuck here without me from now on."

"You can't stay?" asked Amy.

"Why would I want to?" asked Ken. "It's not real, Amy. I need you with me in the real world. You must make a choice. Are you coming with me or not? They were only putting me under for two hours, so I won't be here much longer. We only have this one chance to make this work."

Ken was trying to be patient because he could clearly see that Amy wasn't herself. She seemed delusional, and he was at a loss as to how to reach her and help her make sense of things.

She is incredibly smart, so why can't she see this for what it is? Ken asked himself in silence.

Carson could see the struggle and offered some advice. "It is possible that she has been stuck in my world, trying to conform to it, for too long. Before, she was stuck in your world, and I think she was okay because you two were lost in love together. My guess is the best place for her would be her home. I think when you helped her redo so much of it, that it became a place of refuge for her."

"And just where are we?" asked Ken.

"I don't really know," replied Carson. "I've had many thoughts about that myself. When I hear you refer to the real world, I just think of it as the other world, because this is as real as anything has ever been to me. Wasn't it real to you?"

"Yes, I guess," said Ken with uncertainty. "So what's your

theory on where we are?"

"If coma patients don't produce brainwaves indicating dreams, then that must be ruled out," answered Carson. "So perhaps we're on another plane of existence. Perhaps we're between life and death. Perhaps we're in purgatory, or perhaps... our souls just have to have a place to exist no matter what and we all found each other and created this place ourselves... just out of the ether and it's nothing more than that... just our souls... which would literally make you guys soulmates! Did you know that scientists have tried to pinpoint the soul in the human brain and body? They've never had any luck finding it, but some have theorized that it exists in the form of an energy field that uses our cells to communicate... sort of like a soul network. And if we are each a network of energy, does it not make sense that our networks should be able to communicate with each other? I think that might be how we exist here together."

"I can't imagine a better answer to that question, except why the hell weren't you that forthcoming with information before?" asked Ken.

"I was very afraid of you," said Carson meekly.

"Seriously?" asked Ken. "Why?"

"The first time I was induced into a coma, just to see if I could prove my theory and communicate with Anna, I woke up in a pitch-black room with one overhead light. It was a bit frightening, and it took a lot of effort on my part to even figure out how to change something basic, like turning on a light. I found Anna, and before they awakened me, I began to figure out that I could change anything, like being in complete control of a dream. Anna had been in this state a lot longer and could never really grasp how to change things. When I came in for the second time, I began creating the farm you now see, and that became our home. When you first walked up here and I questioned you, you really seemed to have no clue you were somewhere other than your real home. The fact that you awoke, with your creation already in place and never had to work to figure out how to create or do things here, was frightening. I think maybe, because you are an architect, and you probably always dream up things before you make them real... I don't know... really, I don't... but I'm just guessing that might have somehow created an advantage for you. And, your territory, for lack of a better word, butted up against mine and, at will, you two were able to just cross out of yours and into mine. How was I to know that you wouldn't change or destroy my surroundings, my world, or even me? I didn't know you and couldn't possibly know if you were a threat or not. And, for what's it worth, I really felt bad about not doing more for you when she got sick."

"Speaking of that, what about when she was sick?" asked Ken. "What was that really about?"

"Her physical body had pneumonia, and it affected her here," answered Carson. "That still doesn't mean this world is any less real, just that the two worlds are bound."

Ken turned his attention from Carson back to Amy, "Darling, I'm afraid we are running out of time and you are just going to have to trust me. Okay?"

"I don't know," said Amy. "Can I just do everything on my own? I don't like taking help or anything from anyone."

"No," replied Ken softly. "This is just one of those things you can't do on your own. You are going to have to trust me to help. There simply is no other way."

Amy nodded in agreement, then Ken took her hand and led her off the porch, before turning back to Carson and saying, "Your daughter said she's getting married and needs you to wake up and come to her wedding."

"I don't know what kind of shape my body is actually in out there," replied Carson, "but tell her I love her, and I'll think about it."

As Ken and Amy approached the walking bridge to cross the stream, she became frightened of the darkness ahead. Ken held her hand tight and said, "I have you, and together, we've got this."

They crossed the bridge, and darkness faded into light, and the neighborhood began to shift and morph back into the beautiful homes they once were. They walked the streets together, hand-in-hand, and Amy began to perk up and return to her normal self, mostly.

"Why do you love me?" Amy asked in a very serious tone.

"You're everything to me," replied Ken, "and there's nothing I don't love about you. I take you how you are, and I'll always love you if you just let me."

"We're almost back home," she said with a smile and her childlike voice.

"Home is where we are, as long as we're together," replied Ken.

They entered Amy's home and waited a bit, talking and holding each other. It wasn't long before the whispers began, and ghostly figures entered the room.

"I love you, Amy," said Ken, looking her right in the eyes with his hands on her shoulders, holding her firm. "And you have just one shot to get this right, so please come with me."

"I love you too," replied Amy.

"Hold on to that," said Ken, "and do everything you can to hold on to the feelings you have for me and let go of everything else. Just let go of everything else. Follow the whispers, follow the ghosts, follow our love out of here, okay?"

"Okay," replied Amy meekly, but Ken didn't hear it. He was gone.

Ken awoke in the same hospital bed he had faded from in his mind, two hours earlier. Disoriented, he struggled to stand. Janice grabbed one side of her brother to help stabilize him and asked firmly, "A little help here?" The male orderly grabbed the other side of Ken.

"Where are we going?" asked the orderly.

"Room next door!" stated Janice with authority and pointing the way.

As they all entered Amy's room, they could see her just lying there, still in a coma. Ken pulled away from his support team and grabbed Amy's hand while placing his other hand on her head.

"No, no, no, no, nooooo," said Ken with tears rolling down his cheeks.

"Please, Amy, please," Ken begged. "Please come back to me. Please wake up. I can't go on without you. I need you. Please. Please. Please. I love you so much."

Everyone looked on, as they could see the hope slipping away in Ken's eyes.

"Come on, Lucy," asked Ken softly and playfully. "I really do need you to wake up for me, and come back to reality, with me."

And, with that, Amy opened her eyes.

Acknowledgements

I would like to thank Pauline Harris for the edits and helpful suggestions, and Darah Patterson for the graphic work and formatting.

I appreciate my friends: Shane Martin, Tom Corbin, Mark Sanders, and Brian Adams, who put up with me when I was MIA from normal life, and consumed by all that lead me to this project.

And 1432 to the one I'll never be the same without. It's been genuinely difficult to face life without you. Maybe, just maybe, we can be reunited in a different life.

And to Corinne… I simply don't know how the hell you put up with me… I admire your angelic qualities and know you're more than I could ever deserve. Thank you for being there when I needed you the most. More than anything, I hope you find the happiness you're searching for as no one deserves it more than you.